THE RAGE WITHIN

the Bitter Root Series by

DINA

Ink Trails Publishing Inc.

The Bitter Root
The Rage Within by DINA

Ink Trails Ink Publishing
P.O. Box 291541
Tampa, FL 33687
www.inktrailspublishing.com

Library of Congress Cataloging-in-Publication Data

ISBN-10: 0692370781
ISBN-13: 978-0-692-37078-0

Printed in the United States of America

Cover Photograph: Admiring with Myrie Photography
Book Design: Kenyatta Harris
Publisher: Ink Trails Publishing Inc
First Printing: February 2015

Acknowledgements
SPECIAL THANKS

Firstly, to my Heavenly Father, Jesus Christ who makes all things possible. I am in awe of His greatness.

To my family. Thank you for your continual support, insight, and most importantly – love.

To Darcel Smith, you have no idea how our friendship for the past fourteen years have made such a positive impact in my life.

To my business partners and Sister-Friends, A.W. Myrie and Shan Mahogany – you ladies are my literary aces. Thank you for the laughs, critiques, and the sisterhood that was developed during our monthly writing sessions. We did it!

To the people who know the craziness that goes on inside of my head, yet call me friend...this is for you.

The Bitter Root Series

Dear Reader,

I never dreamed that when I penned my first book, *Rewriting My Story*, and introduced you into my world, that I would be taking readers through my life's journey. Filled with several personal experiences and lessons that I've learned thus far, in my first book I'd aimed to encourage the reader to identify the source of their bitterness and to use it as a catalyst for life-changing and positive experiences. As a result, I've received an overwhelming amount of responses and stories from readers who have experienced similar events in their lives as well. I had no idea that my story would become a source of inspiration and motivation for so many people. My amazing readers have asked for more and so for them, here's book two of the Bitter Root series – *The Rage Within*.

This go-around, I wanted to take you on an adventure in this fictitious approach. In *The Rage Within*, you will be introduced to an intelligent and sophisticated woman named, Angelica. In the story you'll learn about her bitterness that stems from a hurt so deep within, it soon manifest into rage! There are no limits to what she will do. Things couldn't possibly get any worse than hiring a hit man to kidnap your own sister – or could they? For the hopeless romantics, I didn't forget you! There's a little bit of steam to fog the pages, but ultimately this is a story of redemption.

I should also note that Angelica is an extreme version of my younger self. A great deal of the way she processes certain situations are very similar to the ways I use to operate. She takes revenge, anger, and hurt to a whole other level. Many times there's no sensible rationale to rage, perhaps that's one of the reasons why the scripture reads "And don't sin by letting anger control you. Don't let the sun go down while you are still angry." (Ephesians 4:26 – NLT).

I invite you and the others who're brave enough to embark on this journey, to come along for a literary ride on this epic adventure.

Enjoy!

Contents

Prologue

There is something seductive about revenge, Angelica Devina Hunter thought as she stood in front of the full-length mirror. Her target was Devin O'Conner, the man who her mother claimed to be her father. He was the one responsible for breaking her mother's heart, which ultimately led to her untimely death. Accusing her mother of being unfaithful, O'Conner kicked her and their unborn child out of their home with nothing more than the clothes on her back. He shortly married another woman and eventually had children.

O'Conner should have believed her! Angelica knew how much her mother loved him. Despite his cruelty towards her, she never lost hope that one day he would realize that she never wronged him and that even until her death; he held the keys to her heart. This hope was the reason she never married, even when the opportunity presented itself numerous times. Her mother always said "my heart belongs to Devin; he's my one true love. Believe me Angel; daddy will come back for us."

But he never did.

Angelica held back the single tear that was beginning to form in her almond shaped eyes, the only feature she and her mother shared. Her mother, a Caucasian, fell in love with the half African-American, half Italian man she'd met while attending Yale University. She was in her junior year, majoring in English, while he was a senior majoring in Biomedical Engineering. According to her mother, it was love at first sight.

Leaning against the mirror, Angelica could vividly recall her mother's account of how they met...

Cynthia Hunter looked at the man who had caused a stir in the coffee shop located just a few blocks away from the campus. Joe's Coffee Shop was her favorite place to be, especially when she needed to get away from the demands and pressure of being the daughter of one of the most prestigious professors at the university. It seemed that everyone adored and admired her father, Professor Christopher Avery Hunter. Although the shop was a short distance away from the university, those who frequented the quaint shop were not students; rather, they were local profes-

sionals. Students seem to gravitate to another coffee shop just two blocks north of Joe's, but Cynthia simply loved the atmosphere of her favorite shop.

Joe's was not your traditional coffee shop. Every table was assigned a theme, honoring many historical figures. Artists, politicians, religious leaders, and other dignitaries were honored with a booth dedicated to them. Cynthia's favorite booth was the Shakespeare. What person in their right mind did not appreciate the works of Shakespeare?

Her table, like the others, was dressed in a white rectangular linen cloth. And at the center of each table was a sign with information regarding the featured guest of honor. Cynthia looked at her sign which read "The Great William Shakespeare; pre-eminent dramatist." Below the header was a brief biography of Shakespeare as well as his list of works. It did not matter how many times Cynthia visited the shop; she enjoyed reading the wealth of information provided on the single sign.

Sipping her hazelnut-flavored coffee, her attention returned to the man who now was placing his order with the cashier, who obviously was enjoying the view as well. Who could blame her? Even Cynthia was captivated.

Normally, Cynthia would be fixated with the view outside of the window. And what a view it was. There was a bed of colorful flowers near the entrance of the coffee shop, which only enhanced the beauty of the sunny morning. The sky seemed bluer than normal and the sun a bit brighter. This was what dreams were made of. But today, the man speaking with the cashier was invading her dream.

Simply put, the stranger who caught her attention was jaw-dropping, mouth-watering, head-spinning gorgeous. And to top that off, his presence exuded sexiness. He stood at a commanding six-three, wearing a pair of faded jeans and a white collared shirt that accentuated his muscular physique. His black wavy hair was cut short and hi-lighted his dark complexion. This man was simply...

Embarrassed, Cynthia looked down at her coffee cup wondering how she could be so affected and enticed by a man she'd never spoken to. Convinced she was acting like an immature schoolgirl, she shook her head in hopes of snapping back to reality. There was no way, she could even consider being with this mystery man. He was causing such a stir. It appeared that the women in the diner were enjoying the view, while the men were upset with all the attention he was getting. Although he wasn't the first mixed-raced person to come to this shop, this was the first time a man of color commanded the attention of the room with simply a smile. And what a smile it was. The stranger's teeth were pearly white. He must have not been a frequent coffee drinker. Cynthia, being a connoisseur of coffee, knew that there was no way his teeth could've been so white if he was a habitual coffee drinker. And she was a testament of that.

Cynthia then began examining his lips. His full lips were shaped as a heart. She thought lips like that didn't exist; she's only read of lips like that in the romance novels she leisurely read from time to time. But unlike the men in the novels, this man was real. She closed her eyes and imagined him walking towards her, and without a word taking her hand to stand. He wrapped his arms around her waist, flashing that dashing smile, and kisses her. Cynthia was unsatisfied, so she wrapped her arms around the stranger, demanding more of him. His hands began to inch lower and then...

"Oh snap out of it girl!" Cynthia demanded herself. "You don't even know him and people wouldn't approve, especially daddy." Cynthia had witnessed the cruelty interracial couples had endured on campus. She knew that what people, especially her father expected from her was to marry someone within her race. Her father had his sights on Dr. David Berry, who'd recently graduated from a medical school in Europe. By no means was David unattractive; however, Cynthia was not drawn to him. Perhaps it was because he treated people, namely her, as inferior beings. David did not like the fact that she was opinionated and had her own dreams. According to him, a woman's place was in the home. Just thinking of him made Cynthia frown; he was a pompous idiot.

"Hello. Are you here with anyone?"

Looking up at the man who interrupted her thoughts, Cynthia could not help but to admire the mysterious stranger now standing in front of her. What was the mystery man doing here? Was he inviting himself to sit down? Why here? Why with her?

After moments of silence, he began to smile, showing his pearly white teeth and the single dimple that formulated on his right cheek. After a few more moments of silence, he decided to sit in the chair opposite of her.

"Hi, I'm Devin. Aren't you Professor Hunter's daughter?"

Finally finding her voice, she responded "Yes. I'm Cynthia."

"It's a pleasure to meet you Cynthia." He replied, widening his smile and extending his hand towards her.

It was obvious that the on-lookers were not too pleased with the two of them conversing. Some were green with envy while others were probably uncomfortable with seeing a Caucasian woman enjoying a cup of delicious coffee, with a man whose complexion was just as delicious. What began as a simple introduction, led to hours of great conversation. He told her of his aspirations of becoming a biomedical engineer and his desire to develop a monitoring system that would transform the medical field. He spoke of him being an only child and that his parents, his mother of Italian descent and his father who was an African descent, were both well known dentists in New York. He explained the importance of him making his parents proud. Cynthia told Devin that like him, she was an only child and that she understood the pressures of making her father proud.

She'd lost her mother when she was six years old and her father ensured that she would had the finer things in life, more importantly, an Ivy League education. He wanted her to become a professor, although she wanted to become a writer. So she decided that she could achieve both by majoring in English. After their conversation, Devin escorted Cynthia back to campus. During the short walk, Cynthia knew that she'd fallen in love with Devin and no matter how un-accepting people would be of their relationship; they would be together – forever...

Angelica punched the full length mirror, masking the pain in her heart with the pain that she now felt on her fist. She refused to cry anymore; she'd done enough of that when her mother died three years ago. It was at her mother's deathbed, as she watched her mother take her last breath that she vowed to make Devin O'Conner pay for his actions. Her mother may have had a forgiving heart, but Angelica was not as naïve and foolish. It was time for Devin O'Conner to have a taste of his own medicine. And she would start by getting close to him, destroying his precious company, and the family that replaced both her and her mother in his life.

She'd spent the last three years building a name for herself as a Bioinstrumentation Lab Coordinator at the local state college. Her job was coordinating or interfacing all medical imaging, medical devices, software, tissue and cell engineering, drug discovery, pharmaceuticals, genomics, and bioinformatics research projects undertaken by her department. Although she despised the fact that like her father, she was a biomedical engineer, she enjoyed her field of work. She could have easily taken the position as the Senior Research and Development Engineer, but passed on the chance when an opportunity to work at O'Conner Biomedical Research and Design, Inc presented itself.

Her father's multi-billion-dollar company was in need of an experienced engineer to lead in conducting a top-secret electro-mechanical medical device that some are predicting would change the face of medicine forever. She was shocked and pleased when she received news that she was hired for this position. This was quite a feat as countless engineers and researchers were contending to be part of this historical event.

Tomorrow, when she began her new job, Angelica would implement her plan. She would make Devin O'Conner pay for what he did, and make sure that she brought honor to her mother's name. He was going to get what was coming to him, even if it meant his life.

Certain battles are not meant to be fought....
Or are they?

ONE

"The day has finally come and it's time to make him pay" Angelica mumbled to herself as she took a final glance at the cracked mirror.

She decided to wear her favorite black pencil skirt, with a fitted blue-collared blouse. To add a little character to her wardrobe, she adorned herself with a pink and blue scarf, which she considered to be a bit edgy, considering everyone she saw during the initial tour of the facility wore a business suit. To maintain a professional look, Angelica decided to wear nude colored pantyhose and a pair of black pumps. Her hair was pulled into a traditional bun, hiding the true length of her hair, which she detested. Her hair reached her tailbone and was unbearably thick. Often times she'd considered cutting it into a bob, but never went through with it, remembering how much her mother loved her hair. Angelica could still clearly hear her mother say, "Angie, your hair is a constant reminder of God's glory on your life. Why on earth would you ever want to cut your glory?"

Satisfied with her appearance, Angelica headed to the kitchen for her favorite meal of the day – breakfast. Growing up, breakfast time equated to family time. It was during breakfast, Angelica and her mother discussed several matters and topics. They'd often time laugh about their crazy neighbors, or would discover new things about each other. For instance, Cynthia once wanted to become a singer, but her father did not believe it was a suitable career for his daughter. This was one of the many reasons Cynthia never discouraged Angelica from exploring several of her interests, no matter how unique or strange they were, as long as it did not affect her school work.

Angelica completed her meal of dried toast, scrambled eggs, two slices of ham, and a large cup of black coffee. Sipping her cup of Joe, Angelica reflected on her mother's account of the man who she'd fallen madly in love with. What a pity; love never brought forth anything but heartache and pain. Unfortunately, her mother found out the hard way. But Angelica was too smart to fall for that trap again; she knew that true love did not exist – a lesson she learned from her relationship with Tyler. He taught her that men did not know the meaning of love; lust and rage were their masters. Tyler also taught her that men could not be trusted with her heart. And quite frankly, she was content with that. Eliminating the emotional aspect of the relationship made life so much easier. This ensured that she would not be subjected to the pain, hurt, and disappointments that she often witnessed her friends go through, especially her best friend Aleena.

Aleena constantly went through a vicious cycle when it came to the men she dated. Although she was brilliant, and a well-known professor at the local university, she was drawn to men who were needy and sleazy. These men would either use her to pay their rent or use her for sex. Yet, Aleena still had hope that one day; she would meet Mr. Right. "What a shame." Angelica voiced to herself before taking another sip of her coffee. Her best friend's previous relationship was with a guy who did not need any financial support from her. He appeared to genuinely like her; some may say that he loved her, but Angelica knew better. A few months into the relationship, Aleena discovered that he had three kids by three women and was sleeping with another while in a supposed relationship with Aleena. *Who has time for men? There are more important things to focus on...*she thought.

"Mission Destroy Devin O'Conner," Angelica whispered before placing a sinister smile on her face. She drank the last gulp of coffee, stood, and headed towards the sink with her plate, utensils, and cup at hand. She simply disliked a dirty kitchen, let alone a dirty house. This was one of the many attributes she gained from her mother. Angelica often believed that in another life, she would've been an excellent professional organizer or planner.

She liked things to be in their respective place. She was meticulous and detail oriented. Perfection took time and she could attest to that. Even with planning her revenge on her father, she was thorough and focused.

After her mother passed, Angelica changed her surname from O'Conner to Hunter. Hunter was her mother's maiden name. She no longer wanted to carry her father's name, although she did keep her middle name, Devina. She figured that since she rarely used it, her middle name was insignificant. According to her mother, when Angelica was born, Cynthia sent a letter to Devin informing him that he was now a father. She simply provided him the first name of their child. His response to the letter devastated her mother...

Never contact me again! And it would be wise of you to not claim this child as mine. I will not have my reputation tainted by a whore's child.

But even on her deathbed, Cynthia believed that he did not write that letter. She claimed that it had to have been someone else. When Angelica asked her who could possibly do such a thing, she simply said, "No one worth mentioning, but just know that your father loves you and would never refer to you as a whore's child." It was apparent that Cynthia was delusional. If he loved her, then he would've come for her. What a pity – to love someone who didn't love you back.

After straightening up the table, which served as the centerpiece of the kitchen, Angelica grabbed her purse and keys, and headed out the door. In her garage was her pride and joy. There she marveled at the black sapphire colored Bentley that she purchased for herself. It was her birthday gift. Although she knew nothing about cars, what she did know was that these cars looked great, was expensive, and that with this car, she'd be the envy of most people – especially her male counterparts. She took great pride in knowing that she paid for the car on her own.

After a few more seconds, Angelica got in her car, pulled out of her driveway, and headed southbound towards her new job. Had it been under different circumstances, this job at O'Conner Biomedical Research and Design would have been a dream come true. The pay was great, the benefits were astounding, and the staff gave the impression that they were genuinely happy to be a part of something that would benefit patients. They were fools to believe that Devin O'Conner cared about anyone, other than himself.

Noting her anger, Angelica decided to turn on the radio, allowing the music to soothe her soul. She settled for WYUD 91.5, which played a mixture of classical music and jazz. Luckily, between the hours of 6am – 10am, the station only honored the greats of classical music. The local station opened the top of the hour with Julius Fucik's *Entry of the Gladiators*. Angelica laughed, thinking of how appropriate the title of the selection was as it related to her. She was ready to fight, but she couldn't help noting how jubilant the song was. *Fucik should've titled the number something else.* Instantly frustrated, Angelica searched for another channel and settled for another classical station. This time, her car was filled with the dark chords of Prokofiev's Romeo and Juliet: Montagues and Capulets. This was more appropriate to the mood in which Angelica was in. After a few more selections from classical greats such as Bach, Handel, and Verdi, Angelica pulled into the parking garage of her battleground. It was time to impress and dazzle Devin O'Conner. She had to get close to him and do so quickly. Doing so would set in motion her plan of destroying his company, his reputation, and more importantly – the family that he claimed. It was time to give her mother the peace that she never had due to the rejection she endured from Devin O'Conner. It was time to put an end to this once and for all.

Red flags overshadows logic when the heart is open.

TWO

O'Conner Biomedical Research and Design was unlike any other building she'd ever seen. Most research facilities were either associated to local universities near or on the campuses of the respective schools. Rarely did Angelica find a research facility of this magnitude, to be a standalone facility. She had to admit that the structure was superb. No, that was an understatement. It was absolutely magnificent. This building was located on eighteen acres of land and was 40,000 square-feet with the exterior walls engulfed with windows. Oddly enough, it was impossible to see through the windows from the outside. The building was surrounded by uniquely shaped hedges as if cut by Edward Scissor Hands himself. Near the east section of the building there were additional hedges, symmetrically shaped with several aqua colored benches lined along the walkway. Never in her wildest imagination would she ever imagine benches to be the color of water and placed against bright white walls. *Wow. Simply...amazing.* This added an elegant touch to the already beautiful property. "Such a shame, because this place will go down in flames," Angelica said as a devious smiled crept across her face.

During orientation, she was informed that she would join a team of researchers who were working on developing artificial lungs. Competitive research companies were also working on this; however, it was believed that O'Conner would be the first to achieve such a feat. If the team was able to accomplish this, O'Conner Biomedical Research and Design would not only leave a stamp in the medical field, they would be given additional resources to continue future endeavors. Unfortunately, this would never happen, if Angelica had anything to do with it. Such a shame.

Angelica walked through the double doors and was taken aback by the atrium. *Was this a research facility or a museum*, she thought to herself. There were several pieces of abstract art strategically placed throughout the area. In the center of the reception area was a cascading waterfall. To the left were six aqua accent chairs, which complimented the majestic feeling brought about from the waterfall. To the right was a white L-shaped receptionist desk with a frosted glass panel located on the front of the desk. Angelica noticed four security guards strategically placed throughout the atrium. They all wore black suits and had an earpiece. *They must think they're part of the secret service or something*, Angelica chuckled. They began to gawk at her. Ignoring them, Angelica headed towards the receptionist.

"Hello...umm...Ms. Jones" Angelica smiled, noting the metallic name tag. "I'm Angelica Hunter. I was instructed to ask for Mr. Nathaniel Kingsley. It's my first day at work..." Angelica could not understand her sudden nervousness and why she was rambling.

"Yes. Ms. Hunter; Mr. Kingsley is expecting you." The receptionist began, "...and call me Diana," she smiled.

Her smile was contagious; Angelica couldn't seem to wipe the silly grin that now adorned her face. Diana paged Mr. Kingsley and then instructed Angelica to sit in the waiting area. There, she noted a small table with several copies of the latest issue of the *BioMed Digest*. She decided to thumb through a copy as she waited.

"Ms. Hunter?" a man with a distinctive voice snapped Angelica out of her thoughts. *Wow. What a voice?* It reminded her of the late soulful singer, Barry White. Angelica looked up and gasped; gorgeous was an understatement. The man who stood with his hand extended had to be at about six-two, well built, and had silky-smooth-dark-chocolate skin. Yummy. And oh those lips. There's so much she could do with those lips... "Ms. Hunter? Ms. Hunter?" – Waving in front of her, trying to get her attention – "Ms. Hunter, are you alright?" the man seemed concerned.

"Oh. Yes sir. Just a little nervous," she lied. *How embarrassing was that?* Angelica thought; it was very unprofessional and now he probably thought that she was weak.

The stranger smirked, extended his hand and said "Believe me; everyone was nervous on their first day. I'm Nathaniel, but you can call me Nate."

Returning the gesture, Angelica responded "And you may call me Angie."

Angelica was surprised by what she'd said. No one, not even her best friend, was allowed to call her Angie. That name was reserved for her mother alone. But here she was, willingly becoming comfortable with a stranger.

"Well Angie," he interrupted her thoughts, "let's get you to your new home." Nathaniel escorted her to the elevator. When they reached their floor, she followed him down a narrow corridor. Unlike the other area in the building, the corridor was simple. There were no ornate décor to adorn the walls; just your simple white walls, which created a simple and clean and surprisingly comfortable atmosphere. Suddenly, they came to a stop. Nathaniel opened the door and escorted her in. "Welcome to your new home, Angie." There he goes again with that dazzling smile and the sexy way he said *Angie. Get a grip of yourself!* Holding her composure, Angelica simply responded, "Thank you Nathaniel."

"Please, call me Nate." He said with a slight frown on his face. "I figure since we're lab partners, we don't have to be so formal." *Oh no! He is going to be a major distraction.* Shaking her head, Angelica was concerned as her attraction towards Nathaniel was strong. Luckily, she knew it was just a fleeting infatuation. Men were incapable of love; they only knew how to woo, charm, manipulate, and destroy. That's the one thing she learned from her father and it was time for him to have a taste of his own medicine.

"Well, Nate, I guess you can show me around our home." Angelica said with a smile turning her attention back to Nate.

Laughing, Nate responded "Yes ma'am. Afterwards, we will meet with Mr. O'Conner; he's looking forward to seeing you."

Angelica couldn't contain the smile that broaden. She was elated to know that her opportunity to meet Devin O'Conner had finally arrived.

Life's journey has only just begun.

CHAPTER
THREE

The clock seemed to be moving slow! *At this rate, a turtle could have done two laps around the laboratory, stop for a break, and resume its quest around the room! Geesh!* Angelica had seized the opportunity to become acclimated with her work station; she also met with many of the staff that would be working alongside her for the duration of the project. Not knowing what to do for the next 20 minutes, she decided to go to the restroom. She wanted to look impeccable for Devin O'Conner. To her, it was important to never look less than perfect when it came to the man who fathered her. She wanted him to know that she was fine without him and that it was his lost for not wanting her. She was beautiful, successful, and would be a great asset to his company. *A great asset? You're supposed to destroy him, not help him!* "Get a grip of yourself!" Angelica commanded herself. With a quick touch up of her makeup and a straightening of her outfit, she took a deep breath, and headed back to the laboratory.

By the time she reached the lab, Nate called her name from behind. Turning, she observed him speed walking towards her. Not sure why he was urgently approaching her, Angelica responded "Yes, Nate. Is everything ok?"

Without slowing down he said "Hurry, you're going to be late for your meeting with the boss."

Confused, Angelica responded, "No I'm not. We still have 10 minutes before the meeting begins."

Finally reaching her, Nate said "Exactly. If you're on time, you're late; if you're early, you're on time. It will do you well to remember that." Grabbing her elbow, Nate guided Angelica to the conference room.

Sitting in the conference room, Angelica wondered if this was what a myocardial infarction felt like. *I really need to get back to the gym*, she thought to herself. Taking a deep breath, she straightened her attire as much as she could and waited for the arrival of her enemy.

Thirty minutes later and Devin O'Conner had not arrived! *The man had some nerve*! In an attempt to not display her anger, Angelica took a deep breath and examined her well manicured hands to occupy her time. Finally after an additional ten minutes lapsed, the door opened slowly and a gentleman emerged from behind the door. There was something about his appearance that felt and seemed familiar. *Where have I seen him?* Angelica just couldn't put her finger on it, but she was certain that she'd seen him before. He looked like a no non-sense type of guy. *And he was rude! How do you not address people when entering a room?* Interrupting her thoughts, Nate finally spoke, "DJ is everything ok?" *Why is everyone informal around here?* Angelica wondered.

"No. Something came up at the lab in Japan," the stranger responded firmly.

"Anything I can do?" Nate casually volunteered.

"I'm not sure, but I will let you know if we do need your expertise in this matter." As if finally realizing there was another person in the room, *Mr. Personality* greeted Angelica with a smirk and extended his hand to her. "You must be Ms. Hunter. Hello I'm Devin Jr., but you can call me DJ."

"Ms. Hunter, are you ok?" Unable to formulate a complete sentence, Angelica extended her hand to the man who was her half-brother and replied just above a whisper, "Yes."

Saving her from complete embarrassment, Nate interjected, "Your father handpicked this young lady to work on our current project."

With a wide-grin, DJ added "Yes, and he is excited to see what Ms. Hunter has to offer. He's followed your work Ms. Hunter and was quite impressed. He's confident that you will elevate this company's reputation and legacy."

There was something about his grin that appeared to be

questionable. *What is he up to?*, Angelica wondered. Something just didn't seem right. Determined to get a grip and control the direction of the conversation, Angelica squared her back, smiled, and addressed her half-brother. "Mr. O'Conner, I have every intention to meet *your* father's expectations." Not sure why she placed much emphasis on the word 'your', but she digressed – "And I'm sure that my previous work proves this point. I am excited and honored to be part of a riveting project and such a reputable company." Ok, she'd have to admit, that she was trying too hard, but what else could she do?

DJ smirked and with a dry tone said, "I'm sure you will Ms. Hunter. And you are welcomed to recite your monologue to my father at the upcoming company party." And he walked out of the room.

What a jerk! Angelica had to admit that it did seem a bit rehearsed, but he didn't have to be implacable and crass about it. Turning to Nate, Angelica asked, "What party is he referring to?"

He smiled, "The annual company party. You'll receive more information soon. It seems that you were hired just in time. You'll have the opportunity to meet the big man himself sooner rather than later."

Admiring the smoke ring that he produced, he took a deep pull of the cigar. He puffed four smaller smoke rings, desiring to extend the exhalation. His fun was interrupted by the ring tone of his phone. "Say hello to my little friend," the ring tone repeats. He chuckled every time he heard it. *Scarface* was his favorite movie, well; it was right up there with *Godfather II*.

Looking at the caller id, he knew that he'd better take this call. "Yeah Boss." He said as he shifted in his seat. This must be important if the *Big Man* himself, whom he'd never met face to face, called him. He took another puff of his cigar as he listened intently to what The Boss required of him and his associate. Unlike the Godfather, he wouldn't make an offer that couldn't be refused, The Boss was clear – "make him pay." He had a funny feeling about this job, but he learned a long time ago if you wanted to make a name for yourself with this circle of people, you did as you were told – no questions asked.

Once The Boss hung up, he quickly dialed his associate. "Marcus, it's me. The Boss wants us to move now." Knowing that his associate would naturally question the reason for implementing the plan two weeks ahead, he reminded him of who they worked for – "Look, if The Boss wants us to move now, then we move now unless you want your fingers to be chopped." He remembered the day where Little Tony learned the hard lesson of not following The Boss' instructions. His rebellion resulted in three of his fingers cut off and mailed to his girlfriend as a souvenir. He would not end up like Little Tony; his hands were his bread-winners.

His associate finally responded. "Pick me up in about an hour, so we can go over the plan again."

He knew he'd come around; no one wanted to get on The Boss' bad side, nor his. And he'd proven that fact time and again. He'd built a unique reputation by constantly going above the call of duty. He liked adding a special touch to each job, so that the victims as well as his fellow henchmen would always remember him. He was determined to live up to his name – Crazy Bill.

He liked the fact that his street name stood apart from the others, and it gave him permission to live up to his name. This job would be no exception. The Boss wanted his money and if The Boss doesn't eat, then Crazy Bill doesn't eat – and that was not an option. Besides, kidnapping that privilege spoiled brat should be easy.

Experience is a teacher — and in life whatever seems, indeed is.

CHAPTER

FOUR

Angelica was awakened by the sound of her ringtone. Looking at the clock located on the night stand, she became annoyed. Who in their right mind would call her at four o'clock in the morning? Still lying on her bed, she reached for her phone. It stopped ringing. Uninterested, she refused to check her call history. Whoever called will receive an ear-full later, but now, all she wanted to do was get the much needed rest she longed for. As soon as she settled herself, the phone rang again. Unable to keep her anger in check, she snatched the phone and yelled, "This better be important!"

"Angelica? This is Aunt Meagan."

Abruptly sitting upright, Angelica asked "Auntie Tutu is everything okay?"

With a voice filled with sorrow, her aunt replied, "Baby, I'm not sure. I had a terrible dream. I dreamt that you died my Angel."

Taking a deep breath, Angelica said "Auntie, it was just a dream; and since I am having a conversation with you, it's obvious that I am not dead." Trying to keep her composure and suppress her annoyance, Angelica continued, "Now go to bed Auntie; we can discuss this further in a few hours when I am fully awake."

"No! Listen to me!" Aunt Meagan screamed. Successfully getting her full attention, Angelica got out of the bed and stood in silence and waited for her aunt to tell her what was on her mind.

"Angel, I dreamt that a woman wearing a red suit, and black leather gloves had you on your knees. She wore heavy make up as if she was trying to cover up bruises on her face. You were badly beaten. Your face was bloody and swollen, as if you were repeatedly hit with the pistol. You were a terrible sight, barely recognizable. With tears streaming from your blackened eyes, you begged her to forgive you. She laughed and then began to cry. Just when you thought she was going to forgive you, she suddenly stopped crying. Her eyes were as stone; she barely looked human, Angel. She suddenly unloaded her gun on you but she didn't want to finish you off quickly. She wanted you to suffer! She first shot you in your left arm, then your right, then your left leg, then your right... oh Angel, it was horrible!" Then with tears her aunt said "Baby, I don't know what is going on with you, but please be careful; get yourself in line with God."

Angelica didn't know how to react. This dream must have been more horrific than she thought in order to cause her aunt to sound so...pathetic. She decided to calm her down. "Auntie Tutu, shhh; it'll be okay. Don't worry, everything will be alright."

"Baby," her aunt began "seek God's face now."

Rolling her eyes, Angelica knew that this conversation was going to lead to a sermon. And she had no time to hear about her aunt's God. Where was her God when she was raped? Where was her God when her mother was sick? No! She would not spend another minute on the phone with this woman.

"Look Aunt Tutu, I've got to go. I'll call you..."

"No! You will listen to what I have to say; this is a matter of life and death!"

Angelica knew that when her aunt got riled up, she could blow like a horn on a train; hence the nickname, Tutu. Angelica returned to her bed and laid down; she took a deep breath. She knew her aunt had a sermon awaiting her and she would give her aunt the respect she deserved; besides, she was the only family she had.

"Angelica Devina Hunter, you must let go of the past. I know that you're hurt by the loss of your mother. I know that we weren't related by blood, but I considered her as my sister. She embraced me as her sister so much so that everyone believed that we were in fact related. So believe me, we all miss her; however, it was her time. Angel, she'd been ill for some time before she passed. I know that you blame Devin, but you shouldn't. You've got to let it go. Leave your pain and hurt at the Master's feet. I know that life's journey has been tough, but with the help of God, look at you now..."

Your God didn't help me with anything. Angelica thought to herself. Everything she'd gain, she worked hard to get it. There was no way she would give the credit to...

"Angelica, are you listening?" her aunt asked, interrupting her thoughts.

"Yes Aunt Tutu, I hear you," she lied.

"Good. Like I said Angel, if you continue to dwell in your past hurt, it'll fester and ultimately become the root of your bitterness. The Bible clearly teaches us that we ought to "get rid of all bitterness, rage, anger, harsh words, and slander, as well as all types of evil behavior. Instead, be kind to each other, tenderhearted, forgiving one another, just as God through Christ has forgiven you." Bitterness my baby, will cause the rage brewing inside of you to come out, which will ultimately destroy you and more than likely everything and everyone around you. I know that the rage within you is brewing; I can feel it even as I'm speaking. Baby, I know you've felt that God has betrayed you, but He hasn't. And He has not left you. Remember, "He will never leave you or forsake you."

No longer willing to listen to this foolishness, Angelica was determined to end this conversation, "Auntie, don't you worry yourself; it was just a dream. Just pray to your God to dispatch His angels to protect me. It will be alright." She remembered as a little girl, her mother would come into her bedroom to tuck her in. She'd pray the same prayer "Lord, I thank you for the many blessings in our lives, especially the greatest blessing of all, Angelica. I ask that you cover her with your blood and dispatch your angels to protect her throughout the night and during the day. Order her steps so that she would grow up to become the woman you have called her to be...Amen."

"He's your God too; you just need to come back to Him." her aunt stated.

Suddenly becoming angry, Angelica nearly shouted "No. I don't have a God; He's your God! Now, unless it's an emergency, I ask that you don't call me this early again!" Silence filled the air and Angelica realized the magnitude of her disrespect towards her aunt. It wasn't her aunt's fault that she had faith in this God; that's how she was raised – corrupted. She took in a deep breath. "Look Auntie..." Angelica began, "I'm sorry; I should have never..."

"Don't worry yourself about me my Angel. I'm more concerned about your relationship with God. There's deliverance, comfort, joy, and peace in Him. Come back to Him; He's waiting for you with open arms."

Knowing this conversation could lead to yet another sermon, Angelica was determined to end the call. "Yes ma'am. And thank you for the call. I ask that you pray to your...I mean pray to God that He provides a hedge of protection over me." Before her aunt could say anything else, "Auntie, I need to go, it's time for my morning run; I'll check on you later."

After ending the call with her aunt, Angelica decided against the morning run. And since she couldn't sleep, decided to read up on what had been done so far on the project. Ironically, keeping busy was a stress reliever for her. And after the conversation with her aunt, Angelica welcomed the distraction. She couldn't deny the fact that what her aunt stated, began to rattle her. Was this a warning? Should she not seek revenge on the man that killed her mother? Wait a minute – "He killed my mother." Angelica heard herself say. She could feel the anger building up again. Luckily the phone rang again.

"What!"

"Angelica is that you?" It was her best friend Aleena.

"Yes girl it's me. It's five o'clock. Are you alright?"

Giggling, Aleena responded "Yes. Everything is great! I'm just getting in and could not wait to tell you of the magical night I just had with..."

"Wait a minute; you're just getting home? Where were you?"

"I was on a date! And before you say anything, no, he's not like the other guys; he's different."

Rolling her eyes, Angelica could not believe that Aleena was putting herself through this yet again – her friend was a hopeless romantic. It was always the same story – girl meets boy, girl sleeps with boy on the first or second date, boy stops calling girl, girl sees boy with another girl, and girl ends up sitting at home with a tub of ice cream watching "Love and Basketball" – disgraceful. Believing that her friend needed the support, Angelica decided to give Aleena her undivided attention. "Ok Leena, how is he different?"

With eagerness and excitement, Aleena began, "Because he actually wants to get to know me; not once had he even insinuated that he wanted to sleep with me."

That is a first! Angelica thought to herself. Aleena was a beautiful woman. The men she was attracted to were eager to bed her and had no problem making their intentions known. Angelica listened as her friend described *Mr. Knight in Shining Armor.*

"Girl, he is handsome. In fact, handsome isn't good enough. He has Shemar Moore's complexion, Morris Chestnut's body, Taye Diggs's smile and Denzel's swag. He's just too good to be true..."

Yeah, he sounds too good to be true for sure, Angelica smirked. Who was Aleena kidding? Her best friend was known for embellishing. And to think that one man could encompass the well known attractive attributes of some of the leading African American actors of our time was silly. This conversation was ridiculous! Nonetheless, Aleena was a hopeless romantic and such a great person. She deserved to be with a man who would cherish her.

"Angelica are you listening?"

"Oh sorry Leena; what were you saying?"

"I said that he took me to Le Palais for dinner! Afterwards, we headed to the skating ring. Can you believe he rented the entire place so that we could have the building to ourselves? I thought we were reenacting a scene from *Rocky!* It was wonderful. We began talking about our childhood, family, and goals. By the time we were done, it was morning. He brought me home, walked me to the door and kissed me good night. And not just any kiss; he kissed me on my cheek! It was gentle and sweet. He wasn't aggressive like the others; he was a gentleman."

This man *was* too good to be true indeed. What was his motive? *Men like this didn't exist.* Poor Aleena, she was setting herself up to be heart-broken yet again. When will she learn the harsh reality that the man she wanted only existed in the romance novels and the over-sensualized romantic films that occupied her time? Aleena was a professor for crying out loud! Angelica simply could not understand how someone as intelligent and beautiful as Aleena could think so little of herself. *Well, at least she wasn't in love...*

"I think he may be the one."

"What? The one?" Angelica raised her voice. "Leena, you barely know this man. He could be a sociopath, psychopath, or any other dysfunctional "paths" out there! What do you know about him? Where is he from? Where does he work? Leena, you have to slow down!"

Giggling, Aleena responded "Take a deep breath Angelica. I was only joking. I knew you'd over-react. And for your information, he was born and raised here in Connecticut, graduated top of his class at Yale, and he's an engineer and co-owner of some researching company. I know you're concerned, but you can rest assure that I will take it slow. I really think this guy is special and I don't want to rush things."

Angelica was glad when the call ended with Aleena. She normally enjoyed talking to her dear friend; however, considering that she did not get much sleep due to the disturbing call from her aunt and the fairy-tale driven conversation from *Miss When-Will-She-Ever-Learn* Aleena. Now it was about time for her to get dressed and head to work. But before she did that, she would make a call of her own. It was time to scratch the second item off her list, the first being accomplished when she got hired at her father's company. It was time to turn things up a notch and the company's party afforded her the opportunity to do just that.

Rather than blame God ask, "Was is His will?"

FIVE

The next two weeks were eventful. Not only was the team able to develop a practical design of the artificial lung, at this rate, O'Conner Biomedical Research and Design would be able to produce a prototype by the end of the year. This would afford the company to remain as one of the top research company of its kind. But Angelica was determined to ensure that wouldn't happen. For now, she would enjoy the experience and build her resume for when she had to seek employment elsewhere. There was no need to ruin her future along with her father's. She'd worked too hard to become a successful woman and was determined to continue to make a name for herself in this field. But first, she had to get rid of her father.

By the time the third week came along, Angelica was exhausted. Work was beginning to consume her. Her only relief was the myriad of conversations with Nate. What a great guy he turned out to be. During the course of the week, they'd either gone for lunch or had an early dinner. It was through these conversations that Angelica discovered how brilliant this gorgeous man with the Barry White voice was. She learned that Nate, who was also raised by a single mother, had worked his way through school; and diligently ensured that his work would make him one of the most sought after researchers. He spoke of how he used his first check towards a down payment on a house for his mother. And no matter how much Angelica wanted to steer the conversation into a more risqué territory, Nate would ignore her efforts and steer the conversation right back to neutral grounds. *He must be gay*, Angelica thought to herself. She knew she was attractive; rarely was there a guy who would disagree with her assessment. She also knew that they enjoyed each other's company, Nate had admitted to that on their second date. *Wait a minute. Date? Calm yourself Angelica.* These were not dates. These were merely lunch with a co-worker – a very good looking co-worker.

The conversations with Nate were intriguing and thought provoking. Rarely could she discuss literature, the arts, as well as current events with the opposite sex and not feel as if she were speaking to a brick wall. Yet here she was, able to do so with Nate.

The only time the conversation would become uncomfortable was when he would subtly bring up the topic of church. Normally when someone would try to so-called "witness" to her, Angelica would not hesitate to inform him or her that they were wasting their time. With Nate however, she wasn't as forthcoming. She even surprised herself with how forth-coming she was in her admission that she had not been in church for years and that she wasn't interested in doing so now. That did not stop him from inviting her to attend his church anyhow.

Angelica, you've said that you were raised in church. It has been my experience that the most common reason people leave church is because they've experienced a great deal of hurt and pain or they left because they were offended. Your tone and mannerism when speaking about church leads me to believe that you've experienced a great deal of pain. Where is this conversation going? she wondered. He continued... *Well, here's the problem. People often come to church imperfect, believing that everyone else is perfect or has it together or should know better. But they must remember that the only perfect person or being is Jesus. That's why we can stand firm on His word that informs us that He will never leave us nor forsake us. The mistake that people make is believing that once you leave Him, it's over. But that's not true. With God, it's never over unless you decide to completely give up. It's up to you; just rest assure that He's waiting for you with open arms; all you have to do is seek Him.*

After the spiel from Nate, he invited Angelica to church. She promised him that she would consider coming. She surprised herself. Why was she willing to at least consider going to church? Angelica determined a long time ago that God didn't care about her. Where was God during the many nights she actually prayed for Him to heal her mother when the doctors said that there was nothing left to do? If He wasn't going to honor her prayers, why not honor her mother's prayers?

Where was He!" she heard herself yell as her hands formed into a fist prior to hitting the wall. This wasn't the first time Angelica reacted this way. There was something about the sharp sting of pain from a punch on a hard surface that was ironically soothing. As a youngster, she never understood how people could physically harm themselves to mask their pain. But now she understood. There was something familiar about pain and if nothing else, pain was the only consistent and reliable relationship in her life. What would she do without it? The realization of living without her most trusted confidant was rather frightening.

Aunt Tutu often encouraged her to restore her relationship with God, but she just couldn't. She could admit though, that her experience in church was damaged. Unlike pain, this relationship was virulent and toxic. Church was inconsistent; couldn't be relied upon. It was annoying how one moment things could appear majestic and cathartic and yet the next, like the Via Dolorosa. Laughing, Angelica found the comparison to be ironic. Comparing her experience to what had become known as the *Way of Suffering*, the street in which Jesus himself walked while carrying the cross that would be used for his crucifixion, may have been a bit much. But it was because of a horrific act by a so-called man of God that caused a large piece of her to die. The remaining fragment of life dwindled the day her mother died. How could she get herself to trust in Him? For this very reason, conversations like the one with Nate would normally deter her from ever speaking to the individual; however, she admittedly enjoyed her time with him.

Angelica could not help but think that had Nate been just a normal guy and not this super-spiritual being, she could see herself dating him. Not only was he handsome, Nate was charming, intellectually stimulating, and a gentleman – the quintessential Morehouse man. He was the total package. There was something special about Nate. It went beyond the physical, but the spiritual side of him was annoying! She also had to take into consideration that this was her lab partner; it was important that they remained professional and cordial. So for now, she'd let him think that she would consider his invitation to church, but she knew better. There were more important things to do at the moment, like ensure that everything was in place for the party.

As the scent of the black and mild permeated the room, he hung up the phone then laid back down next to *what's her name*. Peering down at his latest conquest, he chuckled. She really thought she could resist him. Oh how he loved a challenge and *Miss whatever her name was*, was no exception. She held out for three weeks before she finally came to her senses and gave in. To his confidant, he was crazy for sure, but to the ladies he was charming – Casanova. Women were a weakness, but a past experience taught him to control his urges, especially when it could affect his work. *What's her name* suddenly shifted and cozied up closer to him; she obviously liked to cuddle. He hated that, but after holding out for so long, she deserved a little tender love and care – at least for the moment.

Taking another drag of smoke, he thought of the call he'd just received. His boss wanted to be sure that he and his partner was ready for the job. This job must be important. This is the third time that she called regarding this job. How hard could a kidnapping be? And why was she willing to pay $500,000 just to capture someone? One thing was certain; in this profession you didn't ask questions that you really didn't want the answers to. The less you knew the better. All that mattered was that he got paid and that he would not be implicated in the kidnapping. He and his partner had already come up with a solid plan, but since there'd be many potential witnesses, extreme measures were required; being precautious was key.

A job like this was a dream come true. He planned on attending some ritzy party which was sure to have local dignitaries and the most elite socialites in the state. He would dress the part and charm his way in to the heart of Londyn O'Conner, the daughter of some famous businessman. From his research, Londyn was rather attractive, which only sweetened the pot. Because of the limited time, he would have to gain her trust and lure her to a private place within a matter of hours. Once he was able to get her alone, his friend would come in, sedate her, lug her off to the van, and take her to the warehouse. Although he was instructed not to harm her, he thought he maybe had to capitalize on this situation and partake in some...pleasure. There was something soothing about manipulation and causing grief; it was better than being intimate with a woman. That realization alone was justification for another smoke and something stronger.

Leaving his lady friend in the bed, he headed to his den where he had a built in bar. His beverage of choice was scotch on the rocks. After two rounds, he seemed to be a bit more relaxed. It was time to call his associate.

"Hey. Our client just called wanting to make sure that we were all set for this weekend."

"Dude, this is the third call about this man. What is up with that?"

He could tell that his associate was just as annoyed with the constant calls, but there was too much money on the line.

"Man, it'll all be over soon. This is an easy job and I know that our plan is solid." The call went silent for a minute before the associate responded.

"So why the call? I was sleeping man."

"Man, I just want us to go over things one more time; we've got to make sure that everything goes according to plan. There's a lot of people that'll be there, which means there's a lot of potential witnesses. We have to be careful; I'm not going to jail again, especially not for something like this."

There was silence again before a response was provided. "I hear you man. I'll be there in about three hours."

Once he ended the call, he poured himself another serving of scotch before sitting on his plush velvet couch.

"Hey baby, what are you doing out here?" The voice of his guest caught his full attention. "Come back to bed." He couldn't help but stare at her standing there; she was beautiful. It was a shame that he would never call or see her again. He couldn't afford for another woman to ever get close to him again. He made that mistake before. Desiree was the only woman who'd achieved the impossible – she earned his trust and then she betrayed him. She couldn't handle his lifestyle and wanted to "save" him from the path he chose. It was because of her that he served five years in prison. When he got out, he made sure that she was handled and was careful to let her live, so that she could re-live the punishment that was due to her. Since then, she had kept her mouth shut.

What's her name cleared her throat. It was apparent he hadn't answered her. But instead of a verbal response, he took a final gulp of his drink, got up and walked towards her like a lion creeping up to its prey and gave her his undivided attention.

Revenge is a roller coaster with no brakes.

CHAPTER

SIX

The evening of the party had arrived and Angelica found herself to be extremely nervous. Everything was in place for the kidnapping, and if all went well, O'Conner would pay a hefty price both literally and figuratively. Secondly, this would be the first time she would come face-to-face with the woman her father married and the daughter that was the apple of his eye. It was well-known that to her father, Londyn O'Conner could do no wrong. The spoilt brat had had many run-ins with the law. She was usually engrossed in the party scene with men who had reputation of being bad boys. She didn't do much with her life after college and intended on being a kept woman. The concept of working for a living was foreign to her, which was odd since her brother took that mantra seriously. It was this revelation that made Londyn an easy target.

Three months ago, a news report had flashed across the television screen about the arrest of Londyn O'Conner, the daughter of famed Biomedical Engineer, Devin O'Conner. The arrest resulted from an altercation she and her boyfriend had with an individual at a local club. They fled the scene before the officers could arrive; however, was eventually pulled over. The arresting officer conducted a search of the vehicle, which resulted in finding cocaine in the glove compartment. *How typical*, Angelica thought to herself. Of course little *Miss Sunshine* claimed that she didn't know about the drugs, nor did she ever think that her beau was a user. Her boyfriend however, implicated her as his dealer and indicated that they often used drugs together. A drug test had proved that she did not partake in any drugs that night.

Although he was willing to incriminate her, Londyn was more than willing to take him back. *What an idiot.* This was the same person who replaced Angelica for the title of "daughter" to O'Conner. It should've been her that was the apple to her father's eye; she should have been his heartbeat, the one whom he loved, cherished, and protected at all cost. The nitwit, Londyn, never appreciated her role, nor had her life serve any purpose, until now.

Angelica glanced at the mirror, assessing her look. For the black tie affair that evening, she'd decided to wear a fitted black Armani floor length gown that would put Morticia Addams to shame. The elegant draping and full length sleeves accentuated her curvaceous figure, yet remained conservative and classy. It was also imperative that she covered up all cleavage; her goal was to be alluring, without looking like a call girl, at least that's what her mother would've said. Angelica adorned a tightly pulled back bun which showed the length of her neck. And she wore light makeup, enhancing her natural beauty. She looked stunning and she knew it. Taking a final glance, she smirked. She was proud of her plan. Tonight, O'Conner would experience a great loss – like the one he caused her mother. And within a few short weeks, he would experience what he would deem to be the ultimate betrayal. Angelica didn't consider it a betrayal. "I could not be a traitor to Edward, for I was never his subject," she recited. The famed quote by William Wallace was true. Although she was his employee, this point proved moot due to him denying her. There was no allegiance to him. But the challenge would be for him to feel betrayed without knowing who'd so-called betrayed him.

Realizing the time, Angelica grabbed her matching clutch and headed towards her car. The drive to the O'Conner mansion was quiet. Normally, Angelica would play music; however, this time she embraced the silence in hopes that it would cause the rage within her to lessen.

Inhale. Exhale. Inhale. Exhale. The breathing exercise was helping a great deal. The success of her plan required that she remained calm, alert, and astute. Before she knew it, she had arrived at the mansion.

It was of no surprise that the property was gorgeous. The driveway to the valet area could have been a tourist attraction.

The formal landscape design was filled with various type of plants cut to straight lines and geometrical shapes. Directly in front of the home was a cluster of fountains wrapped by an array of flowers.

A valet opened the door for her and was not at all shy about taking a cursory glance of her when she stepped out of the car. She hoped that she would be able to elicit the exact same reaction from Nate. She smiled at the valet, handed him the key to her car and headed towards the stairs leading up to the mansion's door.

There were a number of people already there. Angelica wondered how many employees worked for the company. It was a shame that they would all lose their jobs once the company closed down. Ignoring the thought, she scanned the room in hopes that she would find a familiar face. The orchestra was playing an upbeat medley honoring the great, Frank Sinatra. Walking through the crowd, Angelica could see the lust in the eyes of the men and felt the jealousy oozing from the women who accompanied them. Ignoring their reactions, she saw Diana Jones, the receptionist.

"Diana. How are you this evening?" Angelica began.

With a wide grin she exclaimed, "Why Angelica, you look amazing." Her compliment was comforting; perhaps not everyone was jealous.

"Thank you, Diana. And you look lovely yourself."

They chatted a few minutes before Diana was asked to dance by her husband. The couple looked great together and were in sync on the dance floor. She recalled Diana stating that they were high school sweethearts and had been married for fifteen years. It did not take a rocket scientist to see how much her husband adored her. He could not take his eyes off of his wife. They were so in love. At least it appeared that way. Life had proved to Angelica that looks could be rather deceiving. Determined to find Nate, Angelica began walking through the crowd. From time to time, she would stop on her quest and greet the familiar faces from work as well as introduce herself to the dignitaries that she believed could be of use to her in the future. After walking through the crowd, she was disappointed that she had not seen Nate. *Where was he?* Come to think of it, she had not seen any of the other members of the O'Conner family either. *How strange.*

"Lillian, can we discuss this later? We need to join the party." Devin O'Conner began, attempting to remain calm. Now was not the appropriate time for his wife to throw a tantrum. He was tired of her shenanigans and wished...he took in a deep breath. This was pointless.

In the last couple of months, their arguments had intensified. They argued about nothing and everything. Tonight's argument began the moment he stepped into the dreadful house. He detested the house, which was the primary purpose of him working late – the supposed reason for the tongue-lashing he was now receiving. He never liked their house. It was indeed impressive; his wife made sure of it. But it felt cold, unlike the home he and Cynthia had established many years ago.

Their home was small, but filled with so much love. They couldn't afford much as they both refused to solicit help from their parents. Cynthia used the little that they had and purchased aqua colored furniture and other decorative items to break the monotony of the plain white walls. Their quaint apartment was home. Devin never forgot the feeling he felt whenever he was at home. He wanted his business to have the same feel, as this feeling was not found in his present house. For this reason, when furnishing his company, he was adamant about using the same color scheme Cynthia used in their home. His company was his home away from home; his reminder of a better time...with Cynthia.

"Dev, are you listening?" Lillian yelled, "Where were you last night?"

Taking a deep breath, Devin wondered why they were going through this yet again. "How many times must we go through this Lillian? The company is working on a major project that requires many of us to work late."

She scoffed at him, "So, she works with you?"

"Lily, that's enough! This is the last time you will accuse me of having an affair. If you as much hint about me cheating, I will divorce you and take everything. I won't even let you leave here with the clothes off your back! Now, pull yourself together and let's go downstairs where our guests are waiting. And when you get down there, you will shake hands, smile, and thank everyone for coming. You will behave yourself or so help me God, I will ruin you."

Silence filled the room. Suddenly Lillian laughed. It was a sinister laugh compounded by her applause. *What was going on?* Devin wondered.

"What a performance, Mr. O'Conner." Do you think that your threats mean something to me? Do you honestly think your idle threats would move me? Let me remind you, Devin O'Conner, you need me. If it weren't for my family's wealth, you would have nothing. You are nothing without me. How many times have we had to bail you out from those loan sharks, hit men, and even the mob? So you see, my dear stupid husband, you need me more than I need you. You are just a pretty face, nothing more. You serve no other purpose to me other than your pretty face and your so-called reputation. Which by the way, had it not been for my father, you would not have. If you leave me, I will make sure that your life, your name, and your reputation is ruined. So if you don't pull yourself together and do as I say, you will be the one out in the streets left with nothing more than the shame you'll have to live with for the rest of your pathetic life." Lillian turned and walked off. She refused to allow him to have the last word, not this time. She was fed up with his antics. She loved him, but knew that his heart belonged to Cynthia – it always had.

How stupid of her to think that she could change that. From the day their parents arranged for them to meet, she knew that he was love-struck and so was she. She was in love with Devin the moment he walked into the restaurant. However, he made it clear that he loved another woman and that he was only meeting her to appease his father. Lillian had hoped that her love would be enough and he would eventually grow to love her. She'd even gone through great lengths to rid him of the memory of Cynthia.

When his father informed her of a letter he received from Cynthia claiming that she had delivered Devin's child, it was Lillian who suggested that he burn the letter and never speak of the letter ever again, not even to Devin. She then sent a letter to Cynthia demanding that she never contact Devin again. Of course, she signed his name on the letter.

With much persuasion, they eventually married and she birthed their two children. But that made no difference; his heart remained in the past. She accepted that fact a while ago, but refused to be embarrassed; not even for him.

Lillian knew that Devin occasionally slept with other women. But he was becoming sloppy; her friends hinted on his extra-marital affairs. She of course denied it, but hated him for putting her in such a predicament. How stupid and reckless could he be? But now that she made her point, there was no need to keep her guests waiting.

Exit... stage left...And, scene...

SEVEN

"Bartender, I'll have a glass of Coca-Cola please" Angelica muttered. She made her way around the room twice and still there was no sign of Nate. Her quest wasn't entirely in vain as she was please to meet Senator Hernandez and his lovely wife. They were well respected by both major political parties and had an extensive track record with regards to serving the community. Rumor had it that the Senator was a presidential hopeful in the next election, which was the primary focus of their conversation. And like the typical politician, he neither confirmed nor denied the rumors. "Well, should you decide to run Senator, you most certainly will have my vote" was the final statement Angelica made before continuing her quest.

Dr. Watts was another dignitary she was privileged to chat with. He was a renowned engineer who revolutionized the way bio-medical engineers conducted bioinformatics and computational research. Most engineers used his techniques when analyzing biomolecules on a large scale, especially in gene expression studies. She knew he was impressed with her knowledge of nearly every paper he had written. Angelica hoped that she made a lasting impression on Dr. Watts as she knew that in a short while, she would be unemployed. Perhaps the good Doctor would be her new employer. Nate should have been here.

"Hey Beautiful." Angelica's heart melted at the sound of the familiar baritone voice. She turned and came face-to-face with the man who constantly invaded her thoughts. Nathaniel Kingsley... her Nate. He was standing before her wearing a fitted black suit with a well pressed white collared shirt and a red silk tie. He was dashing.

In an effort not to appear witless, Angelica responded, "Why good evening, Mr. Kingsley. You don't look so bad yourself. You clean up rather nicely. I was wondering when you'd finally grace us with your presence."

He suddenly moved in closer while widening his smile and whispered, "It's great to know that you missed me, Angie." Anticipating him to step back to his respectful distance, he didn't move, which only caused her to hold her breath.

Angelica was unsure of what to do next. *Should I wait for his next move? Should I continue to stare at him like a love-struck teenager?* Unable to muster up an adequate response, she decided to say the first thing that came to mind "Umm...N-na-te," she stuttered; "Would you like to dance?" *Are you kidding?* Of all the things she could've said, asking a man to dance should have not been it! *A lady never asks a man to dance. What were you thinking?*

Thankfully, Nate did not appear to be offended or disturbed by her forwardness; rather, he smiled, showcasing the singular deep dimple on the left side of his cheek and replied, "It would be my pleasure." He took the drink from her right hand and placed it on the bar counter, replacing it with his hand. Then like a professional dancer, he twirled her onto the dance floor.

Nate had to be one of the best dance partners in the world. It was obvious that he was well versed in traditional ballroom dancing. In that moment, Angelica was grateful that her best friend Aleena had forced her to take a Waltz class. Angelica had fallen in love with the movements and the prestige that came with knowing the dance – she was hooked. She enlisted in several classes and eventually learned several forms of dance. Some of her favorites were the Paso Doble, Cha-cha-cha, Rumba, Jive, and of course the Viennese Waltz.

Nate told her about his day, his visit with his mother and his plans of taking a long vacation upon the completion of the project. "You are an amazing woman." When questioned why he thought of such, he responded, "In a very short period of time, you have brought us closer to the finish-line than any other engineer. And it appears that you are making a lasting impression on the Big Man himself. He noticed her blush with embarrassment. She was grateful when he decided to change the subject. "So how was your day?"

"I had a relaxing day," she lied. There was no need to inform him of her meticulous plan in annihilating the very company and person he esteemed highly.

They danced for an additional two numbers and by then she was tired. "Nate, I don't think my feet could handle another number. I need a moment to catch my breath."

He smiled. "I understand, Beautiful. Let's continue our conversation sitting down." He escorted her to a private seating area, away from the other guests. There they continued chatting about the humdrum of their day and stealing gazes of each other.

––––––––––––––––––

Devin was relieved that Lillian had finally gotten herself together. *She could certainly put on an Oscar worthy performance,* he thought. Less than an hour ago, she reminded him of his pathetic existence and now, she was playing the *I love my husband; we have a great life* routine. She was right! Her family had helped him out of several ruts time and again, which was the reason he couldn't ask for their help now. He'd really messed up this time. When he first looked to start his company, he was denied loans. He knew that he had the credentials. He had worked for a leading researching company where he developed a machine that improved the way the medical community conducted ultrasounds, resulting in 4D imagery. When he was not listed as the leading contributor and researcher on the project, he made the decision to leave the company. Eventually, his company took the title of the most prestigious and reputable researching company in the state. But his success came with a price – a hefty one.

He made a deal with the devil; perhaps not the devil himself, but an evil man by the name of Big Lou. He was a mobster that provided the financial support needed to open his company. When the company began to generate a sizable profit, Devin began to pay Big Lou who died a few months later. At that point, Devin ceased to make payment and moved on with working on flourishing the company. He also gambled a lot; there was a rush in taking certain risks. It also distracted him from the constant reminder of the hold his parents had on him. Now, not only was his parents controlling his life, his in-laws were doing the same thing.

He knew his wife loved him and that only made her pathetic in his eyes. When he was forced to marry her, he tried to convince her to refuse their parents' manipulation by confessing to her that he could never love her; his heart had and would always belong to Cynthia Elizabeth Hunter. *Oh Cyn. Baby, I'm so sorry,* he thought to himself. He regretted how he allowed his father to manipulate him into driving the woman he loved out of his life. It was unforgivable! His father knew that he loved her; his life was consumed with her. She was brilliant, beautiful, and had the kindest soul. But the differences between their races deter his parents' approval, which was ironic considering that his father was African-American and his mother was Italian. He vividly remembered the day he introduced Cynthia to his parents...

The doorbell rang and Devin was eager to open the door for the beauty that awaited him. He was not disappointed once he opened it. Cynthia, his Cyn, was wearing an orange sundress with her hair loosely pinned up, his favorite style. He loved how the style heightened the length of her neck. "Hi Dev. Can I come in?" she asked with the most beautiful smile. She knew the effect she had on him and he had no problems with that. He was happy and she was the main reason for his happiness.

"Come on in Cyn." She walked in, turned and gave him a hug; she smelled so good. Upon releasing her he asked, "How was your flight?"

She giggled her response, "It was fine Dev. Although my father is not too please with me at the moment." He knew that her father was not pleased with their relationship, but he much preferred sustaining a healthy relationship with his daughter.

"I know that this is tough for him, but I'm confident that he will eventually see that our love is meant to be. Come. I want to introduce you to my parents."

Devin escorted Cynthia to the family room, where his parents eagerly awaited to meet the woman their son had often spoken to them about. They were impressed that she was also a student at Yale and that she was well-off financially. This put them at ease as this meant that she was not a gold-digger as his previous girlfriends, looking to make a name for themselves. "Mom. Dad.

I'd like you to meet Cynthia Elizabeth Hunter."

Devin could not believe that his parents who were excited to meet the love of his life were now speechless. Everyone looked at each other dumbfounded. His parents seemed confused. But why? He looked at Cynthia who was obviously uncomfortable and embarrassed. He couldn't stand his parents' rudeness any longer. "Mother. Father. Did you hear what I said? This is the love of my life, Cynthia Elizabeth Hunter." He was sure to place much emphasis on the word "my". She was his. And they should've been happy for him.

Thankfully, his mother finally spoke. "My apologies young lady; we are glad to finally make your acquaintance. I'm Nicole O'Conner and this is my husband, Michael O'Conner. Please do have a seat."

The conversation was stiff to say the least. His father barely said anything and his mother, who was a talker, had very few words to say. Needless to say, Cynthia did not feel welcomed. Rebecca, the housekeeper, walked in and announced that dinner was ready. At the dinner table, things had not improved. Cynthia tried to spark a conversation by asking his parents about dentistry. That all but lasted about fifteen minutes. Once dinner was finished, he escorted her to her car as she planned on staying at a hotel that evening. Once they reached her car, he apologized for his parents' rudeness. He wanted to come up with an excuse for their lack of warmth, but knew that he could never lie to her. "I'm so sorry Cyn. I don't know what on earth that was about."

Covering her sadness with a smile that did not fully reach her eyes she replied, "Dev, it's alright. I'm sure that they have their reasons. Either way, what matters is that we love each other." She always was willing to forgive others and she knew just what to say in tough situations. Cyn was amazing. If only he could be as forgiving. His parents were rude and they had better had a good reason.

"Dev..." she interrupted his thoughts. "Will you join me for breakfast tomorrow?"

Without hesitation, he responded, "Of course. There's no place I'd rather be." He kissed her on the lips, hoping his parents were watching through the window. "Goodnight Cyn. I want you to call me as soon as you make it to the hotel. I want to be sure that you are safe." They chatted a few more minutes more before they bid each other farewell. Once her car was no longer in sight, Devin headed towards his parents house with determination in his stride. He wanted to know what their problem was and it had better be a good one!

"Mom! Dad!" he yelled as he entered the house.

"In here dear" his mother responded.

Devin followed his mother's voice to the family room. "Mother. Father. What was that? Why were you rude to Cynthia?"

His father finally spoke..."Son, when you spoke to us about this woman, you never indicated that she was Caucasian..."

Unable to allow his father to continue any further, Devin interrupted, "Wait a minute. Why should her race be an issue? Did you not marry someone outside of your race? What's the difference here?"

His father took a deep breath, as if he was trying to figure out how he could make his son understand... "Son, you don't understand. We don't have a problem with her race, but the world does. We don't want you to have to endure what we went through in the name of love. There are people who refuse to associate with us due to the fact that we chose to love someone outside of our race. We don't want you to go through the same hardship we had to go through. Why not choose someone more appropriate for you; there are plenty of fishes in the sea."

Devin could not believe what he was hearing. His father was asking him to give up on Cynthia simply because society was not very accepting of them being together. Devin was not naïve to society's ignorance. He'd witnessed several racist acts throughout his life; however, he believed that Cynthia was the one for him. It didn't matter what the world said. Quite frankly, his father was a hypocrite! He chose to love his mother, who was not of his race, yet wanted him to leave Cynthia. And for what? Ignorance? He looked to his mother for support. When she refused to look his way, Devin squared his shoulders and said "Well father, Cynthia is the one I love. I plan to marry her and make her the mother of my children with or without your approval. I love her and she loves me."

Stoically and unruffled, his father sat in his seat and emphatically replied without raising his voice, "You will not defy me!

Leave that woman alone son."

That was all Devin needed to hear. With no other words exchanged, he walked away from the family room and headed to his bedroom where he packed up his belongings and left. He refused to be under the same roof as his parents.

A year later, when he desperately needed money he re-opened communication with his parents. They received him with open arms when he stated that he and Cynthia were no longer together. This was a lie, but he knew that this was the only way he could get the funding that he needed. Several years later, during an unplanned visit from his parents, they discovered that he and Cynthia were living together. And the chaos only enhanced. In the end, his father got what he wanted – Devin and Cynthia were no longer together. Often times, Devin wondered if the photos his father showed of Cynthia with another man were fabricated, but he never got the chance to find out. His anger caused him to act out of character and kick the only woman he'd ever loved, out of his life.

Face the mirror of your past today and regroup for a
much better looking tomorrow.

CHAPTER

EIGHT

"Unforgivable."

"What was that Mr. O'Conner?" Devin did not realize that he spoke his thoughts out loud. Looking at the Senator, be smiled and replied "My apologies Senator, I was simply thinking of the financial contribution we made to your campaign. I was considering matching it should you decide to run for the office of President. But then I thought it too small and unforgiving should I not provide you additional support." Devin was satisfied that he recovered well and on cue Lillian supported this concoction of a story by adding, "Yes, I told Devin that $100,000 was simply not enough." Well, should you decide to run for President, we would definitely want to provide you as much support as possible."

Senator Hernandez glanced at his wife, smiled at the O'Conner's and replied "I know what you're doing you sly dog. I am not spilling the beans on whether or not I plan to run. We have not made a decision and when we have made our decision, we will inform the media. However, we much appreciated your past, present, and potential future support."

Devin went along with this farce, "Senator, it appears that nothing gets past you."

"What was that about?" Lillian asked Devin once they concluded their conversation with the Senator and his wife. "How could you volunteer to donate more money to their campaign without consulting me first? Devin, you know that we cannot financially support their campaign. For the love of everything reasonable Devin, your company may be successful, but you're barely hanging on by a thread, especially with your bad spending habits. We're finally getting to a better place financially. Please don't ruin it due to your ego."

He was fed up with her mouth, but knew she was right. He took in a deep breath and simply stated "Lily, I have it under control. More than likely, Senator Hernandez will not be running for office; he has a good thing at the senate. Besides, by the time the presidential election comes around, my company would have completed its project and all of our financial problems will be over." Devin was counting on the success of this project. If successful, not only would it open doors for other ventures, his finances would be right on track, at least he hoped.

A few months ago, he received a strange call from a man who referred to himself as "The Boss". He claimed to have been second in command to Big Lou. So when Big Lou died, he took over all of his businesses, responsibilities, and debts. The Boss expected Devin to pay him what he owed Big Lou. Devin did not see why he would be responsible for paying his debt to someone he had no business relationship with. Also, the debt was years old! For that reason alone, Devin made it clear that he had no intentions on paying him. The Boss was angry and threatened him. Devin didn't take it lightly and told him that he would press charges if he called again. Of course, he had no intentions of getting law enforcement involved, as this would grant them access to his financial records. The calls did stop until a few weeks ago when one of The Boss' henchmen called stating "Pay up or you'll lose everything." This chilling message had Devin worried, but because he didn't see any merit in his claims, he left it alone. *Things like that only happened in movies*, he thought to himself.

"Dev, let's talk to a few more of our guests before you address everyone," Lillian interrupted his thoughts. He looked at her who looked at him with questionable eyes. "Are you alright dear?" she asked. *Why was she concerned?* And then he noticed the individuals that were nearby. *Of course, this is part of her act.*

He smiled and placed his arms around her waist "Of course, I'm fine Lily. I was simply admiring the view; you look lovely tonight." And then he gently kissed her on the lips. The women around them blushed, even Lillian! *What idiots*, he thought as he guided his wife through the crowd.

"Well played, Devin" Lillian whispered once the people were no longer in earshot.

He leaned over so lovingly to her ear and whispered with a laced tone, "I learned from the very best, dear."

Angelica could not recall the last time she'd laughed as hard or as much as she did with Nate. He was hilarious! Nate recalled for her the time he'd thought he was a superhero. He took one of his mother's towels and tied the edge around his neck. Then he took a pair of her stockings which he cut holes in them to form a mask. He explained how after watching an episode of *Batman and Robin*, he was certain that he could do some of their acrobatic moves. He instantly stood on the couch and attempted to do a flip. He called this experience an *epic failure* as he was admitted to the hospital and had to wear an arm cast for a month! "I love to hear you laugh, Angie," Nate admired. Unsure as to why she was embarrassed, she did not respond. He moved in closer, leaned towards her as to reassure her of his sincerity, "I mean it. It's infectious. You should laugh more often."

Flattered, she smiled and thanked him for the compliment. Angelica desperately wanted to change the conversation because this was a bit much for her. She shifted in her seat which showcased her discomfort. Nate then placed his hands on hers and said, "Don't be shy with me, please. I must admit that I am attracted to you and would like to get to know you better." She looked in his eyes and saw sincerity and...what was it? Love? *There's no way he could love her; he didn't know her,* she convinced herself. But she was intrigued in knowing why he would be interested in her.

Refusing to look away, she asked just above a whisper, "Why? Why are you interested in me Nate?"

"Because I'd be a fool not to be."

Angelica could not believe what he was saying. Had any other man given the same response, she would have laughed in their face. This *Smooth Operator* jazz that he was spilling would have never moved her. In fact, she normally found it quite insulting. This was the kind of nonsense Aleena fell for. Angelica used to fall for liners and zingers such as this one too. But she learned to beware of these things after her relationship with Tyler.

Tyler was a well-educated and prominent attorney who'd swept Angelica off her feet with his charms and charisma. He was gorgeous and women swooned at the sight of him. But he also had a dark side. Eight months into their relationship, Angelica noticed a change in Tyler. She could not pin point what'd triggered the change; however, the change had become quite evident. On their eight month anniversary, Angelica had prepared a meal fit for a king. She decided to surprise him with a romantic dinner for two at his home. She strategically placed scented candles and rose-petals throughout the dining area. To enhance the mood, she'd created a playlist of music filled with ballads and jazz, his favorite genre of music. She expected that night to be no different than the past seven anniversary dinners they had – dinner, music, slow-dancing, cuddling on the sofa while watching a film, and perhaps a little more.

When Tyler arrived home that night, it was evident from his reaction that he had not expected her to be at his house...

"Angelica, what are you doing here!"

Why is he yelling, she asked herself. In hopes to change his mood, she announced, "It's our eight month anniversary, Ty." To her dismay, he became more furious. "And so you thought you could just come to my house and tamper with my property?" The tone of his voice was laced with something more than anger. Venom. Unable to disguise her hurt, Angelica responded, "Ty, we always celebrate our anniversary. And this is not the first time I've surprised you at your home." In fact, they'd often stop by each other's home unannounced since the moment they decided to give each other a copy of their home key. So why was he upset? Assuming he had a bad day, she walked towards him. "Ty, you must've had a long day. Why don't you come to the..."

"Shut up you wench!"Ty not only shouted at her, he pushed Angelica to the ground once she reached out to touch his face.

Stunned, Angelica could not believe what had taken place. Tyler, the man she'd loved and respected pushed her. How could he do this? Why would he do this? Her thoughts were interrupted when Tyler launched towards her. It was then, Angelica's initial shock wore off and she quickly got off the floor and ran behind the sofa. Tyler began chasing her while yelling to her with profanity. He finally reached her and grabbed her by the waist, with her back facing his front.

"Let me go Ty! What has gotten into you?" Her attempts to escape his hold proved futile, so she tried reasoning with him. "Baby, what's the matter with you. Whatever it is, let's discuss it over dinner."

For a brief moment, Tyler appeared to have calmed down; he simply stared at Angelica with what looked to be hatred in his eyes. 'But why would he hate me?' Angelica thought to herself. And then it happened...

Tyler pushed her to the ground. He stood over her and yelled "Next time you decide to come to my home uninvited, I will have you locked away!" Unable to believe him, she whispered, "No you wouldn't. You love me."

With is head slanted and his eyes darkened with profound hatred, he barked "Are you calling me a liar? And who would ever love you?"

Angelica knew at that moment, there was no turning back. She could never forgive him for this moment. In an effort to maintain the little dignity that remained, she began to stand. She intended on gathering her belongings and heading home. But instead she was brought back down with a kick to her stomach. It took her a moment to realize that he had taken off his belt. But when she did come to her senses, it was too late – Tyler was whipping her with a belt.

Angelica could do nothing but scream and raise her arms to block the blows while trying to get up. She needed to escape this horrid ordeal, but was constantly brought back down by his punches and kicks. Tyler finally stopped hitting her. He stood; glaring down at her tear stained face and began unzipping his pants. In fear of what he would do next, Angelica mustered up the strength to get up, but again was brought down; this time, with a fist to her face.

Tyler brutally raped her that night and then purposefully bathed her before kicking her out of his home. Filled with so much shame, Angelica did not press charges. In fact, she never told anyone. She convinced herself, that somehow it was her fault. Perhaps, she should have not assumed that it would be ok to go to his home unannounced, no matter the number of times she'd previously done so. Perhaps, she should had fought him off as opposed to giving up, allowing him to violate her.

A month later, during a routine visit to the doctor's office, Angelica received news that she was pregnant. Although she had not spoken to Tyler since the day he threw her out of his home, she phoned him with the news. He denied that the baby was his, told her to abort it, and hung up the phone. Unable to rid herself of the baby, she decided to keep it. However, a few weeks later, she'd lost the baby. Never again, would she trust a man with her heart; nothing good could come of it

But this was different, she thought. Nate was different. He had provided her a beacon of hope with regards to love. And although his response was vague, it did mean a great deal to her; however, she refused to reveal this to him. Rather than address his statement, she replied, "Nate, I think it's time that we mingle; we wouldn't want to come across standoffish. Grateful that he did not push the matter any further, Nate stood and offered her his hand, which Angelica gladly took.

Lust is a ravenous wolf decked out in white wool.

NINE

ᶜ∿ᵒ

The man in the van released another puff of smoke. He loved the taste of a good cigar. They were parked near the rear entrance of the house along with the various vendors servicing the party. He and his partner purposefully chose a white van with a logo of a well-known flower company. An event of this magnitude was sure to be filled with several floral arrangements to impress the guests. He looked at his partner in crime, "Alright man. Just like The Boss said the target lives in the guesthouse on the east side of the house. I'll go in and wait in the closet until she gets there. Then I'll shoot her up with the needle. Once she passes out, I'll call you. You'll drive around; we'll put her in the van, take her to the hideout, and wait for further instructions from The Boss."

His partner smiled, "this should be easy like Sunday morning." Both men chuckled; the song reference was silly.

Angelica and Nate were in the middle of a heated debate of the latest stem cell research development when Devin and Lillian interrupted. "It never fails. When a group of intellects come together, even at a function such as this, they can never set aside their work." Everyone gave Devin their undivided attention, some laughed at his observation. It was true, even when off work; the team seemed to always find a way to veer their conversation to current events in the medical world. Devin and Lillian officially greeted everyone with a firm handshake, and smiles.

"Hello Angelica. We're glad that you were able to make it." Devin spoke. Angelica was finally facing the man who was the object of her obsession. His photographs had done him no justice; he was handsome. She could see why her mother had fell in love with him at first sight. She wondered if he noticed the similarities between the two of them. Angelica noticed they shared several features, notably the very distinct singular dimple on their right cheek. Did he notice that like her mother, her eyes were almond shaped? Maybe the fact that her complexion was darker than her parents threw him off. *Typical male! He didn't notice a thing*, she smiled before responding... "Thank you for the invitation, Sir."

"Please, call me Devin. And this is my wife, Lillian." Angelica stood before the woman who'd replaced her mother. "Hello Mrs. O'Conner. It's a pleasure to meet you." Angelica was sick to her stomach. She didn't know if she could continue on with the charade. But she knew that she had to pull herself together for the sake of her the plan.

"The pleasure is all mine, Angelica," Lillian began. "Devin has spoken highly of you and the progress that you have made. I am glad to see a woman leading the pack." She winked. Angelica couldn't help the smile that quickly spread over her face. Had they met under different circumstances, Angelica believed that she and Lillian could have been great acquaintances. Lillian seemed to be a strong-minded African-American woman who, although was courteous, appeared to be a force to be reckoned with.

"Mr. O'Conner...I apologize...Devin...I was wondering what you intended to do once we completed..."

"No. No. No.", he interrupted her. "There will be no talk of work this evening, Angelica. Tonight, we are here to simply enjoy each other's company as well as get acquainted with your peers. Please relax and enjoy the evening."

Embarrassed, she responded, "Yes sir." Redirecting her attention to Lillian, she commented on her attire "Lillian, I love your dress. Who's the designer?"

"Thank you, Angelica. I designed this one myself. I hope to open my very first boutique with my custom designs about this time next year." Angelica was both shocked and impressed. Lillian had earned a degree in Accounting, not design.

As if she could read her thought, Lillian answered "I am a numbers person; however, I've always been fascinated with fashion and design. So I decided to merge my degree and passion. And voila! A boutique. And I am doing it all on my own!"

Again, Angelica was quite impressed with her. Lillian discussed additional business ventures she wanted to implement. Angelica discussed her desire to become a renowned engineer. She eventually wanted to open her own research company. Angelica wondered why Lillian did not chastise her for this. Instead, she encouraged her to accomplish her goals. Lillian then began discussing her family.

Angelica hoped that she would be able to avoid this topic. Unfortunately, Lillian wanted to boast on the success of her children. "I am so proud of my children," she began. Junior will surely take his father's company to the next level and Londyn...well; she'll eventually decide which career path would be best suited for her." In an effort not to reveal her slight disappointment for her daughter, Lillian continued, "My daughter has many talents. And for that very reason, it is difficult for her to narrow down her career options."

Angelica wanted to laugh, but who could blame her. A mother often saw only the good in her children.

"So what about you Angelica? Do you have any children?"

Angelica simply replied "No ma'am. I don't have children."

"Well, what are you waiting for? A beautiful and intelligent woman probably has men lining up for her attention."

Angelica couldn't help laughing. She replied, "Very true. But a man can also be burdensome, especially those who are interested for the wrong reason. Life has taught me to be content with being by myself. If *Mr. Right* comes along, he'll have to truly be special."

Lillian smiled and warned, "Well, I've noticed the way Nate has been watching your every move. Mr. Right may be right in front of you."

Angelica giggled. "He seems to be a good man, but I am in no hurry to jump into a relationship with anyone. I also like to keep my options opened."

Something behind Angelica caught Lillian's attention. "Well, it looks like another option is headed your way."

"Excuse me Miss," the handsome stranger behind Angelica began. "Would you care to dance?" Angelica turned to face the stranger. He was strikingly handsome. He stood well over six feet, had a muscular build, smooth caramel skin, and a smile that could melt ice. *Gorgeous!* Angelica was uncomfortable and had intended to turn down his offer when Lillian interjected "She'd love to." Angelica glared at Lillian who smiled and mouthed, "Options."

Angelica smiled and mouthed "Ok." She noticed Nate who appeared disturbed by the stranger. *Men and their ego.*

The stranger offered Angelica his arm to escort her to the dance area. He didn't move with the same fluidity as Nate, nevertheless, he was a decent dancer. "I'm Patrick" he stated.

"Hello Patrick. I'm Ang..."

"Angelica. Angelica Hunter. I know," he interrupted. Angelica was confused. *Who was this man?*

"Don't look so confuse, Miss Hunter," he began. "I'm the man you've...urr...invited to the party."

Angelica became more perplexed. She never invited anyone to this party. "I think you are mistaken sir; I did not invite you or anyone to this party."

He chuckled. "Yes you did. You invited me once you offered to pay me and my associate $500,000 for an umm...assignment."

Angelica gasped. *Why was he here! What did he want?* As if he heard her unspoken concerns, he leaned closer to her ear and seductively whispered, "Don't worry. This is part of the plan. I intend to seduce Miss. O'Conner. I'm sure that I can get her alone." He smirked before he continued. "Once alone, well, you already know. When the job is complete, I will call you from an untraceable phone. Don't bother taking the call; let it ring three times and press ignore. This way, I will know that you received the message. I'll wait for your call later tonight for further instructions. Now, I want you to blush and act as if I just paid you a compliment. It appears that we have an audience." Angelica did as she was instructed; looked around, interested in knowing who her audience was. *Nate!*

There he was. Nate. He did not hide his discomfort in seeing her dance with another man. To add fuel to an already uncomfortable situation, Patrick regained Angelica's attention when he placed his index finger on the right side of her chin and gently moved her face towards his direction. "It was a pleasure to meet you Miss. Hunter. Be sure to check your phone periodically." He then left Angelica on the dance floor as the other couples continued to dance.

Angelica did not know how long she stood there before a familiar voice caught her attention. "Angelica Hunter, are you planning on standing there all night?" *This could not be happening! What other surprises was in store this evening*, Angelica thought. She turned to find her best friend, Aleena standing before her and with...DJ!

Devin Junior's arm was wrapped securely around her waist. Was he the knight in shining armor she spoke of not too long ago? No doubt DJ was handsome, but he was nothing like what she described. He didn't have the features of the sexy actors she listed. Angelica could not help the chuckle that came out of her lips. Aleena constantly stretched the truth when it came to her love interests.

"Hello. Earth to Angelica." Aleena was apparently annoyed by her lack of response.

Angelica cleared her throat. "My apologies Leena," she began. "I don't know what came over me. I didn't know you'd be here."

Aleena enthusiastically stated while holding on to DJ, "Angelica, I'd like to formally introduce you to Devin O'Conner Junior." *Was she kidding? Surely Aleena knew that DJ was no stranger.* Aleena knew where and whom Angelica worked for. It was obvious that she was putting on a show. Oh how she hated when her best friend was so-called in love. Aleena behaved like a love-struck teenager as opposed to a well-educated professor. Her mannerism as well as her vocabulary changed. However, to show support, Angelica thought it wise to go along with her...antics.

"Why Devin, it's nice to see you."

With a smirk, he replied "Really?"

What a strange response, she thought. "Yes. I had the opportunity to speak to your parents; your mother is quite lovely." Angelica smiled in hopes to reduce the tension that appeared to be brewing, but that proved to be impossible when DJ responded – "Interesting."

Interesting? That's all he can say? In a final attempt Angelica replied "Yes, quite interesting. This is a lovely home."

"Thanks."

That was it! Angelica had had enough of his rudeness. And quite frankly, the fact that her best friend did not object to his actions was quite insulting. Angelica was fed up and was determined to let DJ know of this. "Well DJ, it's obvious by your monosyllabic responses that you are not interested in conversing with me. And there's no need for me to pretend that I want to converse with you beyond the workplace. Good night."

Angelica was please with her response. Aleena's facial expression clearly indicated that she was shocked by her friend's rudeness. DJ's expression remained unreadable, but there seemed to be a glimpse of annoyance in his eyes. Angelica began her dramatic exit, when DJ responded, "Bye." *There he goes again, with his monosyllabic answer.*

Like a moth to a flame...

TEN

Londyn was late. She despised these sorts of events. Her parents were adamant about portraying the family as picture perfect. Little did they know they were not fooling anyone. Nonetheless, Londyn had no choice but to go along with the charade, especially after her stint in jail a few months ago. She could not believe Charles implicated her in the drug bust. In fact, she was rather embarrassed that she hadn't noticed what he had been up to. But what caused Londyn the most grief was when she forgave him and took him back. What a mistake! He apologized for betraying her and promised he would never hurt her again – but he did. This time, she was not as forgiving.

Luckily, a drug test proved her innocence. This did not stop her parents from tightening the invisible leash they'd placed around her neck since she was a child. They made her feel like a major disappointment. And although she had a degree, she was nothing like her brother. DJ was *Mr. Overachiever*. He graduated top of his class, helped with their father's business, and was well respected. She on the other hand was constantly scrutinized. Londyn refused to allow the uptight nitwits that her parents were, constantly trying to impress to dictate how she lived her life. She believed in the philosophy – you only live once. And she intended to live life to the fullest, even at the cost of her so-called family's polished reputation.

Londyn entered her parents' home. Oh how she dreaded coming here. She preferred being in her home. She and her brother resided in separate guest houses located on her parents' thirty-two acre property. This was a sure-fire way for her parents to tighten their leash on her; however, Londyn didn't complain. Who in their right mind would turn away from the opportunity of residing in a luxurious home at no cost? She most certainly was not complaining...at least not about that.

Rather than seeking her parents, she decided to head straight for the bar. If she had to put up with the likes of her parents, especially her mother, she would need a stiff drink. "What can I get you ma'am?" the bartender asked.

"Anything that will help me forget that I'm here."

"Yes ma'am."

"With such a wonderful ambiance, why would a beautiful young lady such as yourself rather be elsewhere?" the stranger voiced. Londyn was in no mood for any form of flirtatious banter and *Mr. Need-to-mind-his-business* was about to get an ear full. Londyn turned to face the man who was going to feel her wrath, but was lost for words the moment she saw him. *Mr. Need-to-mind-his-business* was...yummy.

"Hello. I'm Patrick." He extended his hand. "And you are?"

Londyn eagerly took his hand and sweetly announced a bit louder than she'd hoped. "Hi. My name is Londyn. Londyn Samantha O'Conner."

The bartender returned with a glass of tequila. Londyn gladly took the beverage as she knew that she would need something to calm down the internal volcano that was beginning to erupt.

"It's a pleasure to meet you, Mrs. O'Conner." The stranger started to turn away when Londyn grabbed his arm. He inquisitively looked at her.

In hopes to justify her actions, she quickly stated, "It's Miss. My mother is the Mrs."

"My apologies, *Miss.* O'Conner," he leisurely replied. Londyn loved how he placed much emphasis on the word "Miss". "I was unaware that the O'Conner's had a daughter."

Londyn could not believe that there was actually a person in the room who did not know who she was or how she was perceived thanks to her recent shenanigans. "Pardon me," Patrick interrupted her thoughts. "It appears that I have offended you."

Shaking her head, Londyn replied, "Not at all. You've actually given me hope."

"Hope?" He was interested in knowing in what?

She giggled and answered, "Yes. Hope. Until now, I thought all of my father's employees were too wrapped up in his personal affairs and were unfairly judgmental. But you had no idea who I was. I'm glad to know that there is someone who is more concerned about their work than they are of matters that have nothing to do with them."

Patrick chuckled. He was glad that she thought he was an employee. *This job was too easy; it's like taking candy from a baby.*

"And why are you laughing?" Londyn interrupted his thought with a tone that hinted slight annoyance.

"I'm sorry," Patrick began. "I was thinking of how indeed pathetic it is for people to judge someone before getting to know them."

With a sigh of relief she replied "Precisely." Feeling a bit bold, Londyn then asked "Would you like to take a walk with me? I'm really not interested in mingling with these hypocritical-backstabbing socialites.

Offering his arm, Patrick replied, "Gladly."

Angelica was too anxious to remain at the party. Meeting Patrick face-to-face was a harsh reality of what was in the works. She could not understand why she was beginning to regret her decision. It wasn't as if Londyn would be harmed? She would be a little riled up; however, Angelica made certain that she instructed Patrick not to lay a finger on her. He would take Londyn to a warehouse and send a ransom note. Once the media coverage frenzy began, Angelica would anonymously reveal several dark secrets about the O'Conner's. Whether the secrets were true or not were irrelevant. She would make certain that they appeared legitimate. At some point, Londyn would be released, and O'Conner would blame her for all the negative press his family would have endured. Then bam! His company would take a major hit with the failure of their latest project as well as news of extortion. Angelica wanted O'Conner to be viewed as a criminal. In fact, she hoped that he would end up in jail for his crimes. Granted to her knowledge he had not committed any crimes; however, breaking her mother's heart was enough justification for imprisonment.

He was a murderer!

The guilt she had begun to feel quickly dissolved. She was beginning to feel tired and wanted to head on home. But before she left, Angelica wanted to say her farewells to Nate.

Aleena and DJ were dancing to yet another song. The band was awesome, playing an array of upbeat tempo songs from the past three decades.

"Devin, why were you so rude to Angelica?"

DJ looked at the woman whom he'd fallen in love with. He could not believe how quickly he fell in love; this was unlike him. But there was an old saying "birds of a feather, flock together" and he was beginning to wonder whether or not she was "the one."

"Devin!" Aleena caught his attention. "Did you hear my question?"

Unable to lie to her, he apologized for his rudeness. "I'm sorry Leena. I've got a lot on my mind."

Aleena gently touched the side of his face ensuring he knew that he was forgiven. "I asked why you were rude to Angelica."

DJ took in a deep breath; he did not want to discuss *that* woman. In fact, he rather do something else with *this* woman. But the newfound revelation of his love for her forced him to take things slow. He would go at her pace and when Aleena was ready, she'd have to be the one to initiate.

Knowing how persistent Aleena was, he decided to answer – "There's something about her that makes me uncomfortable. I can't seem to pinpoint what it is, but she doesn't seem to be who she appears to be." There. He said it. He wondered what her response would be. Would she despise him? Would she leave him? Would she stay?

Aleena began to laugh. "Believe me, Angelica is 100% authentic. What you see is what you get with her. She never has a hidden agenda; she is the most genuine person I know. I've known her for quite some time now, and I can attest that Angelica Devina Hunter is a..."

DJ stopped dancing and asked, "What did you say her name was?"

Aleena wondered why he was interested, "Darling, I said her name is Angelica Devina Hunter. Why do you ask?"

Unsure of why her name bothered him so much as well as the need to change the subject, DJ gazed into the eyes of his beautiful lady, leaned forward and kissed her. They got lost in the moment and the subject was officially closed.

A touch of jealousy can be flattering, but deadly.

ELEVEN

Nate was sitting alone in the seating area where they previously were. Angelica smiled. The man looked divine. "Hello Nate." He looked at her with questionable eyes. Angelica could not determine whether she should speak or wait for a response. Why was he staring at her as if he did not recognize her? "Nate? Is everything alright?"

He took in a deep breath before he broke his silence – "Who is he?"

He? Who is he? Angelica had to know. "Nate, who are you referring to?"

He stood up and moved closer to her before answering, "The man you were dancing with."

Was he jealous? It appeared so. *But why,* she wondered. "Nate, I just met him. He asked me to dance; you were nowhere to be found, and I liked the song." *Why am I rambling?*

"Well, it didn't appear that way."

Whoa! What is his problem? "Nate as I said, I just met him. And why are you questioning me as if you're jealous?" And then it happened. He leaned down and kissed her.

Angelica could not believe what just happened. Nathaniel Kingsley kissed her on the lips! Stunned, Angelica placed her hand on her lips and stared at him.

"Londyn, you are such a fascinating young lady," Patrick began. And that was an understatement. Londyn seemed to be adventurous. She was a rebel and defiant. She hated being told what to do and made no apologies when she didn't meet people's expectations of her. She spoke of some of the antics she'd pulled simply to get her parents riled up. To Patrick, some of her antics seemed immature and childish; however, according to Londyn, they were done in hopes that her parents would loosen the invisible leash around her neck. She was indeed fascinating, but Patrick knew what he was there to do.

"Patrick, can I ask you a serious question?" Londyn began. Without waiting for a response, she continued. "Why is a man as handsome and sweet as you are, alone?"

Patrick could see that Londyn was serious. *Women can be very stupid*, he thought. They'd just met and already she was throwing herself at him. *This kidnapping definitely was going to be easy.* Patrick plastered a smile on his face and replied, "Who said that I was alone?"

Londyn gasped and immediately looked as if someone had ripped her heart out and stomped on it. Patrick realized she'd misunderstood him. He moved closer, invading her personal space. He wanted her to feel his presence, and remind her that he was all male. He then whispered with a seductively wicked voice, "Londyn, the reason I am not alone is because I am here with you." He broadened his smile to provide some reassurance of what he said. He wanted her to feel special. That was the trick. In order to get her to invite him to her house, she had to feel comfortable and safe.

"Oh Patrick! That was very sweet of you!" she exclaimed.

"No, this is what's sweet..." he kissed her. Londyn latched onto his lips and she knew that she was a goner.

Patrick released Londyn once breathing became necessary. He knew he had her right where he wanted her and decided to take a more direct approach. "Londyn," he whispered against her lips. "Is there somewhere we can go that's more...private?"

Londyn knew what he was asking and to be honest, she wanted the very same thing. Why deny herself the thing that she wanted? *You only live once*, she reminded herself. "How about my place?" she suggested. Patrick couldn't mask his excitement. His smile became infectious, and the moment he saw the smile that crept on the face of his prey, he asked her to lead the way.

"What is that...?" Crazy Bill began to wonder when the sound of the bedroom door interrupted this thought. He was in the closet waiting for the woman The Boss wanted. Luckily, the bi-fold closet door was a plantation louvered wooden door which made it easy to see who was entering the room.

Londyn held Patrick's hand as she guided him to her bedroom. She wanted to seduce him. Entice him. Love him, even if it were for one night. Not ignorant to the fact that they may not see each other beyond that night, she wanted to be sure that they took their time. Londyn began taking off her clothes slowly.

What a show! Patrick was enjoying the performance that Londyn was providing. He knew that his partner was probably wondering what was taking him so long, but he couldn't rush this. No. She had a body of a goddess. *I just might have to taste her after all,* he convinced himself. He stood and began removing his jacket when suddenly the closet door flew open...

"What the heck is going on?" Patrick screamed at the direction of the man holding a gun towards him. *Was this a set up?* he wondered. He looked at Londyn and realized that she had no idea who the man was. She screamed from the top of her lungs before fainting. *What a drama queen,* he thought. "Hey man. Whoever you are, I don't think you want to do this." Crazy Bill had not said a word and quite frankly didn't intend to.

Bang!

Crazy Bill dialed his associate's number. "It's done." He immediately hung up the phone before placing it in his pocket. He then walked towards the bodies and stared at the man he'd just shot. *Everybody wants to be a superhero,* he thought as he shook his head. He then stepped over the body and picked up his prize. There was no need to drug her since she was unconscious. Throwing her over his shoulder, he began walking out the door where he knew his associate would be waiting. As he headed for the door, he noticed a stack of paper and several pens on a small table near the exit. He had a thought... he took a pen and wrote in capital letters – *You got The Boss' money. And we've got your daughter. You'll get her back once he's paid. But if you wait too long, she may not get back in one piece.* There. He figured that should get O'Conner's attention. If not, he'd have to take some drastic and more permanent measures, which would mean only one thing – death.

Repentance should be considered the
8th wonder of the world.

CHAPTER

TWELVE

It had been three days since the party and it was a media frenzy at the workplace. The news of the kidnapping of Londyn had traveled fast. And of course, everyone was on pins and needles. Statistics proved that the likelihood of someone who'd been kidnapped being found alive after 48 hours was unlikely. Angelica avoided contact with most of the staff and engrossed herself with work. But she could not effectively stay focus as she thought of the series of events that took place since that dreadful night...

"Well goodnight, Nathaniel. Thanks to you, I had a wonderful evening." Angelica said before kissing Nate on the cheek and heading home. Although she despised when men were irrationally jealous, she forgave him. Apparently he cared for her and he made that fact known several times throughout the night. Angelica had to come to grips with the harsh reality that she loved Nate. She didn't quite know when it happened. Maybe it was the moment she had heard his voice on her first day at work. Or maybe it was when they'd first had lunch. Perhaps it was during their conversations earlier that night. Either way, she knew that she loved him.

When Angelica arrived home, she checked her phone to see whether or not she had had any missed calls. She'd purposefully increased the volume on her phone after her discussion with Patrick, ensuring that she would not miss his call. However, the call never came. The phone indicated that she had not missed a call. Worried, she wondered, did he go through with it? Maybe something went wrong. She was very worried. What if something did go wrong? Even worst – what if he'd gotten caught? The need to calm down suddenly struck her, so Angelica decided to brew a pot of tea.

Several minutes later, she sat at the kitchen table sipping on the flavored tea. Normally she would add a few teaspoons of sugar, but her mind was in such turmoil that the flavor of the tea was non-existent. The warmth of the tea was what she needed as she waited and waited for the call...

Minutes turned into hours and Angelica was now on her fourth cup of tea. "Why has this idiot not called!" It was more of a statement, rather than a question. She was becoming irritable and knew that she could no longer sit. She was stressed. And in moments such as these, what she needed was a long cold shower.

After her shower, Angelica looked at her phone; again, no missed call. She became weary and it took a toll on her body. She was tired and knew that she had to rest if she planned on going to work. She refused to take a day off in fear that it would make her appear suspicious. Her daily routine had to remain the same. Deciding to call it a night, Angelica went to bed knowing what was waiting for her – a restless night.

The following day, Angelica headed for work even more tired than when she went to bed. Her mind was racing a thousand miles per hour and she could not seem to slow it down. She should have remained home, but knew that it was best that she came. The team had decided to work every weekend until the project was complete. Once she arrived at the facility, she noticed a slew of media outlets, police officers, and investigators who were questioning the staff. She took a deep breath and headed to the elevators, in hopes that she would evade attention upon herself. When she reached the elevator, she pushed the button several times as she noticed a man with a tan coat heading her way. Calm down Angie. Take a deep breath. The elevator door opened just before the man could reach her. "Miss. Miss! I'd like a few words with you," he yelled while speeding up. Angelica ignored him as the elevator doors closed before he could reach her.

Angelica raced to the laboratory where she closed her eyes, placed her hands over her chest and took a deep breath. She was glad that she avoided a potential interrogation. A few seconds passed before she sensed that she was not alone. She looked to find Nate staring at her. "Nate." She said sighing, relieved to see him.

"Are you ok, Angie?" he asked as he rushed to her side. She looked at him and melted. She was so glad to see him. He immediately wrapped his arms around her and asked again if she was alright.

To put him at ease, Angelica finally answered, "I'm fine, Nate. I simply needed to catch my breath. What is going on? There are police officers everywhere!"

Nathaniel held her tighter and said "Londyn O'Conner is missing."

Angelica knew that a reaction to the news was crucial. She wiggled herself from Nate's embraced and stared at him. "What do you mean she's missing? Where did she go?" Angelica knew these were silly questions; however, in moments such as this, one had to show some level of naiveté.

He escorted her to the lab station and informed her of the news. "The news broke a few hours ago about Londyn. According to a ransom note found in her home, Londyn has been kidnapped. Apparently Mr. O'Conner owes some "Boss" a large sum of money and they plan on holding her hostage until he pays up."

Boss? Angelica was confused. Was that the code name Patrick used? Why did he leave a ransom note? That wasn't a part of the plan. Hoping to sound genuinely concerned, she asked, "Why her? Mr. O'Conner owed the money. Why not go after him? Why did they have to go after his innocent daughter?"

"That's what we'd all like to know," Nate replied.

A million questions came to mind. She wanted to know if they knew anything. Trying to narrow her questions, she looked away. Thankfully, Nate had mistaken her reaction for a sign of sadness. "Angie." He whispered, as he pulled a chair next to hers. He stroked her back and crooned, "Everything will be alright. There are detectives searching for her. We all have to remain positive." She turned towards him and gazed into his eyes. There was so much warmth there. And then the impossible happened....she cried.

Tears began to stream down Angelica's face. When the time

came, how would she be able to let him go? She knew she was a monster and therefore, unworthy of his love. But there was a part of her that was still hopeful. Again, mistaking her reaction, Nate tried to comfort her. "It's okay, Angie. Everything will be okay. As soon as they identify the man that was with her, they'll probably be able to determine his associates and pinpoint her location."

She was curious. "Man? What man? Was there a witness?"

"No. There were no witnesses. However, they found the body of a man in Londyn's bedroom."

"Who's body?"

"Some Neanderthal who portrayed himself as an employee. It was the very same man you danced with last night." And there it was; another glimpse of jealousy. Ignoring his reaction, she probed him to provide more details. "Apparently he flirted with several ladies last night and was finally able to convince someone to share their bed with him. Unfortunately it was Londyn. According to the officers the man's name was Andrew and he had a long rap sheet. It's believed that while he and Londyn were alone in her bedroom, someone entered her home."

For some reason, Angelica was actually relieved to know that her plan had failed. But who on earth had kidnapped Londyn? Then the irony dawned on her – whoever this "boss" was must have also planned for her to be kidnapped the same evening that she had intended on having her kidnapped. She could not hide the smirk on her face.

"What are you thinking?" She'd forgotten that Nate was there.

She looked at him, placed her hand over his and replied "I was just thinking how blessed I am to be alive. Had I fallen for Pat... I mean Andrew's advances; Lord knows what could've happened. Thank God for wisdom." Angelica shocked herself with her response. She actually thanked God! Nathaniel appeared pleased and suggested that she "properly" thanked him...at church.

The following day, Angelica woke up and rummaged through her closet. She could not believe that she had agreed to attend a church service. But she had no other choice. She had placed herself in this predicament the moment she so-called, thanked God. And now here she was trying to figure out whether she should wear a suit, a two-piece ensemble, or a dress. She finally settled on an ankle length turquoise maxi dress and a pair of pink stilettos. Satisfied with her choice, Angelica headed toward the bathroom.

Angelica arrived at New Birth Apostolic Church five minutes late. The church was massive and beautiful. The structure was art deco, heavily using symmetric and geometric forms. The building was octagonal and was reinforced by massive pillars which provided a cascading effect throughout the exterior of the building. When she entered the main entrance of the church, two women who obviously did not understand the concept of personal space greeted her. The ladies introduced themselves and welcomed her to the church, while offering a hug in which Angelica felt obligated to take. Oh how she hated this.

One of the ladies then escorted her to the station where visitors were asked to provide their personal information. Angelica knew exactly what would happen if she provided her information. They would call her the following day, tell her how happy they were that she'd visited with them, and then try to convince her to come back again. Not this time. She would not fall for the trap. Angelica provided her name and email address only. Once she completed the questionnaire, she was then escorted to a seat in the worship center.

Praise and worship was wonderful. It reminded Angelica of the happier times she'd experienced in church before..."It doesn't matter," she reminded herself. "You have to move on." The praise team had just completed their first selection, which was an up-tempo song that she did not recognize. And now they transitioned into a more slow-tempo selection. Again, Angelica was unfamiliar with the song, but she thought the lyrics were beautiful. It spoke of the redeeming power of God's love. It was what she needed.

Angelica suddenly felt compelled to raise her hands and close her eyes while basking in the peaceful presence felt in the atmosphere. Everything felt right; here was the place she needed to be. As the song continued, she began to say a silent prayer "Lord, please make this right. Forgive me." It was all she could muster before a floodgate of tears were opened. The singers began singing yet another song, one that Angelica was familiar with. It was a song pleading that the Lord would make her over. She began to sing as much as could, but often times could not complete the phrase of the song as guilt consumed her. She was hurt, ashamed, and wanted to finally let it go.

Reality struck Angelica. It was truly time to let go. She'd believed God had caused her plan to fail and she thanked Him for it. She prayed that Londyn would be found soon. Upon the closure of the song, a man ushered the audience into corporate prayer. He began to pray for physical, emotional, and spiritual healing. He then prayed for individuals who had a special need. Finally, through his prayer, he stressed the importance of salvation and prayed that the Lord would touch the hearts of all who were lost. When he completed his prayer, the audience applauded and thanked the Lord in advance for answering their prayers. It was beautiful.

The service was filled with great music by the choir as well as the typical humdrum of a church service which included a Meet and Greet segment, announcements of upcoming events, and testimonies. But the highlight of the service for her was the preached word, which ironically was titled "Vengeance belongs to God." The pastor began to read Romans 12:18-19:

"Do all that you can to live in peace with everyone. Dear friends, never take revenge. Leave that to the righteous anger of God. For the Scriptures say,
"I will take revenge; I will pay them back," says the Lord."

The message was eerie as it addressed the affects of revenge, not only to the person seeking the revenge, but to the individuals in their lives. Revenge had a tendency of causing a ripple effect of hurt and pain. He further explained how the burden and responsibility of revenge had been taken away from the child of God and placed in God's hand. The preacher further taught that God had a purpose in allowing certain things to take place in their lives; however, if we trusted in Him, he would work everything out in order to fulfill His purpose. Finally, he addressed the importance of showing mercy to those who'd wronged you. He cited Matthew 5:7:

"God blesses those who are merciful, for they will be shown mercy."

At the closure of the message, the pastor invited the congregation to come to the altar if they were struggling with past hurts that had festered in their hearts. Angelica began approaching the designated area located near the stage, as the Pastor continued to encourage those individuals coming forth to let go of their hurts and forgive those who'd wronged them. "It's time to leave it all in God's hand."

Dear Rapist,
Only MONSTERS find thrill in harming people.
Sincerely,
Your Victim

THIRTEEN

"It's been three days and this fool still hasn't paid The Boss," Marcus quipped. Since the party, the abandoned warehouse beyond the state-line became home to him and Crazy Bill. They were instructed to stay put until they received a call informing them that payment had been made. Unlike Marcus, Crazy Bill knew how this generally worked. The police would encourage O'Conner to wait a few days before offering to pay the ransom, while they searched for his daughter. The smart cops would suggest that he at least offered to pay ransom in an effort to set them up. But The Boss was no idiot. He wanted the money wired to an offshore account. By the time they'd try to track them down via the accounts, the money and them would've already been gone. This plan worked before and it would certainly work now. This was Marcus' first kidnapping, so he didn't know any better.

"Calm down," Crazy Bill began, "This is how things work. Relax, watch some television, and enjoy the food." He paused before making his next statement. "Or you could do what I did and have a taste of that chick. She's really tasty."

Marcus was uncomfortable with Crazy Bill taking advantage of their hostage; they were never instructed to touch her or as he put it *taste her*.

"Man, I'm not down with that. I'm here to do a job and that's it."

"Suit yourself," Crazy Bill shrugged. "That's more of her for me then." And speaking of more of her, I think I'll go have another taste right now." He stood and headed towards the area of the warehouse where they had tied up their hostage. His phone rang and he knew that it could only be one person... The Boss.

"Yes Sir," he began, "Do you have further instructions?"

The voice on the other end of the line was quiet, yet distinctive as he responded, "O'Conner has not sent the money."

Crazy Bill knew that a reaction was not what The Boss wanted. In fact, he knew that a reaction would only rile the man. The Boss constantly emphasized the importance of not showing any emotions; he said it made you weak and an easy target during an interrogation.

The call went silent. Crazy Bill looked at his phone to see if the call had disconnected. It hadn't. He placed the phone to his ear and waited in silence for further instructions. He often times wondered if the reason The Boss constantly took his time whenever he spoke was to test the patience of his associates. Internally, he chuckled. That couldn't be it, as Crazy Bill proved numerous times, that when it came to The Boss, patience was second nature.

A few moments passed before The Boss spoke again. "It seems that it was a bit presumptuous to assume that O'Conner would get the initial message. But it appears he requires further encouragement." Crazy Bill admired how his boss phrased things. Unlike other Dons he'd met, The Boss was well educated, like Michael from *The Godfather*. Perhaps that was the reason for his admiration towards him. "I think," The Boss continued, "that we ought to send him a more permanent message." The call went silent for a few more seconds. Crazy Bill glanced at his phone once more and realized that the call this time had ended. That was another thing he admired about the man; he knew how to make a dramatic exit.

"More permanent message," he echoed. Crazy Bill rubbed his chin and wondered what permanent message he should send. Perhaps a photo of the hostage. Whatever he decided, he would make sure he had fun doing it.

Londyn wanted to die. She didn't know exactly how long ago she'd been captured, but guessed that it had been at least two days.

She couldn't remember much of what happened before she woke up tied to a chair, in what appeared to be an abandoned warehouse.

The warehouse was grim, gloomy and cold. Most of the windows were barred up with timber, yet the smell of dampness filled the air like an infection. A few feet from Londyn was a dilapidated wooden table in which layers of dust clung to its surface. On the table sat a house lamp, the primary source of light.

Although much of Londyn's memory was blurred, she remembered fainting at the sight of the man with the gun. He had several scars on his pale face, which was overshadowed by the knife wound that began from his right temple to the bottom of his chin. His grotesque features were heightened by five missing teeth and his breath reeked of old cigar and decay. He was vicious and cruel. He was the very reason she wanted to end her life...

When she'd woken up, his partner offered her a peanut butter and jelly sandwich and a glass of tap water. She was grateful that they had at least fed her; this meant that they wanted to keep her alive. Refusing to untie her, the man fed her the meal. When she had taken her last bite, he stood and said "Good girl. Don't worry, as soon as your father pays us, we promise to let you go."

"What are you doing?" The man that was previously in her house yelled! "We don't comfort the hostages!" His partner immediately apologized for his actions and headed towards him saying, "It won't happen again," before walking away. She was left alone with the man who appeared to be running the whole operation. His facial expression was unreadable, but his eyes told a different story. There was something sinister in the way he looked at her. The longer he stood there staring at her, the darker his eyes became and then she noticed a smile forming on his lips. What was he going to do? Londyn was terrified. She knew he was up to no good.

The man crept towards her, like a predator stalking its prey. His movements were slow and deliberate. He began unbuckling his belt, and then he tampered with his zipper. What was he doing? she thought.

Londyn closed her eyes, praying and hoping that she would wake up from the nightmare. Several seconds later, she sensed him standing directly in the front of her. He smelled of body musk and cigars. She then felt the blade of a knife alongside her face. She panicked as she thought of the scar that adorned the full length of his face. She feared that her fate would mirror his.

"Open your eyes," he commanded. Shaking, Londyn did as she was told. She'd hope that he would have mercy on her once he saw how horrified she was.

He didn't.

The man cut the ropes that bound her and grabbed her by the hair, throwing her down on the ground. Londyn yelled and tried crawling away, but was silenced the moment his foot stomped her. She couldn't breathe; couldn't find a voice. Why is this happening to me? She couldn't fathom why anyone would want to harm her with such a degree of cruelty.

The man reached down and began cutting her clothes off with his knife. The blade accidentally pricked her on the left thigh when she attempted to move. "Don't move!" he yelled before his fist made contact with her face.

This was really happening.

The man quickly removed his pants and got on top of her. In a final attempt to avoid her fate, she tried to push him off. When that didn't work, she used all of her might to punch him several times. Again, her efforts were ineffective.

Wam!

Londyn felt the open palm of her assailant's hand across her face. The pain was beyond excruciating. It was then she knew that her fate had been written. Mentally she began to drift away, blocking out what was about to take place. When he realized she no longer was putting up a fight, he whispered in her ear, "Good girl" before licking the full length of her face. "You taste so good" were the last words she heard before completely slipping into utter darkness.

When he was finished, he stood over her, admiring his work. He tapped her once on the leg with his foot, wanting to get her attention. She didn't move a muscle. He tapped her again, this time with more force. Londyn shifted her head to face her attacker. Tears began to crease down her once beautiful, now bruised face. And her eyes were blood-red.

In spite of her appearance, he smiled. Kneeling beside her, he gently brushed away the tears that continued to flow. "You're so beautiful," he began "even with tears. Do you know that? You are so beautiful." Londyn's tears turned into sobs. "There. There. Don't cry. It'll all be over soon. Daddy will pay up soon. Don't you worry." He leaned down further and gently kissed her on the lips. Gasping for air, she opened her mouth in between the sobs, not realizing she'd provided an opportunity for him to deepen the kiss. And so he did. With that she knew that he was ready for yet another taste of her.

Londyn recollected the numerous amounts of times the man had raped her. She was beginning to lose faith that her parents would ever find her... alive. She took a deep breath when she heard the familiar footsteps approaching. She was certain that he was coming to violate her again. She looked down and listened as the sound of his steps increased. *He's getting closer*, she thought. And then, it stopped. Londyn refused to look up at him. So he grabbed a fist full of her hair and pulled her head back. She gazed into his eyes and saw only pure wickedness. "So it appears that your father refuses to pay your ransom." He yanked her hair even harder. "It's probably those cops telling him not to pay. Well, we're going to have to send them a louder message. But first..." He began to untie her and then stood in the front of her. "Get up!" She stood in fear as to what he might've done if she had disobeyed. But because her legs were so weak, she fell to her knees. "I knew you couldn't get enough."

He kicked her to the ground, causing her head to make contact with the chair prior to hitting the concrete floor. But he didn't care. Instead, he unzipped his pants and got on top of her. "I'm going to make this quick. The Boss expects me to do my job."

He raped her. And though quick, it was more forceful than before. After he was done, he performed his ritual. He stood over her, admiring what he'd done. This time though, things were different. As he looked upon her frail body sprawled out on the floor, he reached into his pocket and retrieved a phone, then took several pictures of her. "Now let's send a permanent message," he said before pulling out his pocket knife and a pair of black leather gloves.

"Hey man. I need you to print the photos from this phone and drop it off to O'Conner's with this," Crazy Bill instructed. He handed Marcus the large envelope containing a lock of Londyn's hair. He usually would cut off a finger or an ear, but he couldn't convince himself to do that. She was just too beautiful. And he didn't want to damage her. He figured the photographs could easily be interpreted as harm being done to her. Of course, he didn't see it that way. She should've been happy that she was still alive.

Every action is said to have an equally measured
reaction...be careful.

CHAPTER
FOURTEEN

Three days and between the media frenzy and constant inter-rogation by investigators, the team could not remain focus on their project. Everyone seemed to be on pins and needles, hoping and even praying that Londyn would be found alive. The discovery of An-drew's body made Angelica questioned her own safety. She'd hoped that her plan wouldn't have resulted in a casualty; however, she ad-mittedly was glad that not only had her plan failed, but she could not be implicated in the capture of Londyn since her hired-gunman was now dead.

Angelica saw the need for a break. "Team, it appears that with all that has taken place, we could use a break. So how about we take an extended lunch and be back in let's say...two hours." All of her team mates seemed to be pleased with her suggestion. Angelica wished Nate was there as she would have wanted him to accompany her to lunch. *Oh well; it's his loss*, she thought as she grabbed her purse and headed out the door.

Lillian O'Conner took another sip of tea before placing the trembling cup on the table. For the past three days, she had lost her appetite. She just wanted her baby back. *Lord, please help us find my*

Londyn, she prayed silently. She'd never considered herself to be a spiritual person, but at a time like this, who else was there to turn to? *Lord, if you help us find her, I promise to go to church. And this time I'll be consistent* she continued before her tears consumed her yet again.

"Hey," Nate began, brushing the tears from her eyes with his right hand and holding her hand with his left. "Please don't cry, Lilly. They'll find her. Shh....don't cry." Lillian struggled to stop the tears as she did not want to draw any more attention from the customers in the café. She was thankful for Nathaniel. He was such a great friend. He was always right there when she needed him; readily available to offer his shoulder to lean on. When she'd phoned him upon Devin's confession to his association with the mob, which led to the capture of their daughter, he opened his home to her. He promised not to mention her whereabouts to anyone, especially not to her soon to be ex-husband. In fact, he went on with his daily routine in order to elim-inate any suspicions that she was with him. But this morning, when he saw the self-inflicted emotional torture she was going through, he insisted that she needed some fresh air. That was just the kind of man Nathaniel was, she thought – gentle, kind, and loving. He was noth-ing like the man she'd married; he wasn't greedy, irresponsible, and a worthless specimen. She hadn't informed him of her plans to divorce Devin as yet. Telling him now may've caused some forbidden reac-tion to take place. Besides, she had to focus on her baby now. Lillian quickly grabbed a napkin when she felt the tears fighting to return.

Angelica entered the café and was immediately drawn to the area that appeared to be the point of interest to the customers. *Lil-lian O'Conner...with Nate*! They were sitting in the rear of the café and seemed too close for comfort. Angelica then noticed Lillian cry-ing. *He's only comforting her*, she thought. She felt a bit guilty for her insensitivity; and besides, Nate could be trusted. Lillian looked under-standably devastated. And to think that she could have easily been the very cause of her pain. No mother should ever have to worry about the well being of their child. Angelica was so thankful for not being the cause of Lillian's tears. She decided to approach them and offer whatever support she could.

"Excuse me..." she began as she reached their table. Nate and Lillian glared up at her, appearing as if they didn't want to be both-ered. "I apologize for intruding but, Lillian, I just wanted to say that I am sorry to hear about Londyn. I am trusting and believing that God will step into this situation and bring her back home safely." The only response Lillian could muster up were staggering sobs and tears.

Nate stared at Angelica with unreadable eyes. *What is his problem,* she wondered? *Did I say something wrong?* And then it hit her, He didn't attend church service on Sunday; was he with Lillian? She shook her head, erasing the thought of it from her mind. She was being silly.

"Nathaniel," Lillian interrupted her thoughts. "I need to go to the restroom." Nate gave Lillian his undivided attention and assisted her to her feet. She looked frail, unlike the statuesque woman she appeared to be at the party. There, she was confident and a pillar of strength. Now, she was distraught and needy. Lillian walked in the direction of the restroom. When she was completely out of sight, Nate sat back down.

Several moments passed and he hadn't said a word. He barely looked at Angelica. Unable to deal with the silent treatment, Angelica spoke. "Nate, is there something the matter?"

With what was obviously annoyance in his eyes, he replied, "You shouldn't be here, Angelica?"

A wave of hurt struck her, and she could not stop the feeling she felt by his response or the cold way he sounded calling her by her first name. She had to know why he was being so cruel. "Nathaniel, the café is opened to everyone. If you wanted some privacy with..."

As if appalled, he glared at her and said, "We don't need privacy; why would you think such a way. Now that remark was really petty of you, Angie."

Embarrassed by the whole ordeal, Angelica squared her shoulder, "Well Nate, I simply wanted to provide some support, but it's quite evident that I am not wanted here, so I'll just leave you alone." As she turned to leave, he captured her wrist. She turned in haste to scold him for his action, but when she gazed into his eyes, it revealed something she hadn't seen before...admiration.

"Please; have a seat." Angie sat in the available seat directly across from him as Nate continued. "Look Angie, the reason why you shouldn't have come over here is because you're a distraction. How am I supposed to provide any emotional support to Lillian, who is a dear friend by the way, with you in the midst? There is just no way on this earth I could not be distracted by your beauty, that smile, your eyes..." *Wow. He's such a romantic,* Angelica thought.

Nate apologized for his actions and then abruptly changed the subject. "So Angie, I thought that you planned on visiting my church yesterday. Where were you?" he inquired.

"Actually Nate, I did show. I sat in the far back of the church." Wanting to prove her presence in the service, she began to recite everything that transpired "...and the word was awesome! The preacher spoke on redemption." Angelica saw a confused look on his face. "What's the matter, Nate?"

"Are you sure you attended *my* church? I'm asking because my pastor spoke on the importance of being in the will of God."

Angelica emphasized, "*No*, he spoke on redemption. Pastor Charles..."

"Wait a minute." He interrupted. "Pastor Charles? My pastor's name is Pastor Mane. Are you sure you attended New Birth Deliverance Church?" Angelica giggled as she realized the confusion. "Nate, I must have gotten the name mixed up. I went to New Birth Apostolic Church. And I rather enjoyed the service. I intend to visit their midweek service as well. Why don't you join me?" She hoped that he would say yes. This was something that they could do together. Nate was about to give his answer when Lillian returned...

Nate stood suddenly, again giving her his undivided attention as he helped her to her seat. She appeared much calmer. Angelica didn't know what to say to provide her with some level of emotional support, so she just sat there in silence. Thankfully Nate had other plans. "How are things at the lab, Angie?" She smiled in appreciation prior to responding. "Everyone is doing their best, under the circumstances of course" He nodded his understanding. Lillian remained silent. *This could've easily been my fault*, Angelica thought to herself. The guilt of her potential involvement began to overwhelm her. She decided that it was time to leave. As she stood she announced her departure. "I'm so sorry, but I have to get back to the laboratory. Again, Lillian, I will continue to pray that God would help them to find your daughter." She leaned down and gave her a kiss on the cheek before heading out of the café.

Salvation is free; the choice is yours.

FIFTEEN

It was Wednesday and Angelica had been looking forward to mid-week service. The past few days were gravely stressful. There was no news on Londyn and people were beginning to believe the worst had happened. Refusing to accept that Londyn was dead, Angelica whispered a prayer, "Lord, please bring her home safely."

Angelica pulled into the church's parking lot, parked her car and swiftly headed toward the main entrance. "Hello, Sister Angelica." One of the ladies who'd welcomed her during her first visit spoke. "I'm so glad you've come again." Angelica appreciated her warmth; however, she was eager to head into the service. She was looking forward to the great worship and another life-changing message that was sure to take place that evening. Already, New Birth Apostolic Church felt like...home.

The singers and musicians didn't disappoint. The worship portion of the service was dynamic! They led the congregation in a worship medley of hymns that centered around Calvary. Angelica recalled how her mother use to love those types of songs; she'd often referred to them as "blood songs" as the messages behind them spoke of redemption and the saving power found through the ultimate sacrifice Christ made when offering his own life as a ransom for sinful humanity. The harmonious sound and sincerity in their worship was awe-inspiring.

After the medley of songs, the moderator led the congregation in corporate prayer, in-which he spent the majority of the time appealing to God to set divine appointments in their lives in order for them to reach those who had not made the decision to be saved. During the prayer, Angelica thought about Londyn and her family. "Jesus, save Londyn. Help her to come home. And give her family a peace that surpasses all understanding." Her prayer wasn't as lengthy as the moderator's; however, she believed that God had heard her petition as well. Her mother would often say "It's not about the length of your prayers baby, but the fact that you pray." Her mother would be proud now of her renewed faith and veneration in God. Angelica reflected back on the message regarding redemption that was preached during her first visit. She was eager to find out what the pastor would preach on that evening. Angelica's query was short lived when he approached the pulpit.

"Praise the Lord Saints," he addressed the congregation. "Tonight, I'd like to speak on Biblical Salvation..."

From what Angelica understood, salvation meant the process and lifestyle that one should live in order to have eternal life in heaven. If an individual did not follow that process, hell would be their portion. She was taught as a child that salvation simply required a person confessing with their mouth that they had sinned, then asking God to forgive those sins, and finally, accepting or proclaiming Jesus Christ as their personal Lord and Savior. In doing so, they would have secured a spot in heaven. She never quite understood the concept. To her it seemed like it was easier to get saved, than to get a divorce. Inside she believed that there had to be more to it, but she'd never argued because it appeared to be the belief of everyone around her, including her own mother. However now, the pastor was providing a different stance on the process of salvation.

"Now I know that religious traditions would have you to believe that all you have to do to be saved is accept the Jesus Christ as your Lord and personal Savior. And yes, in order to be saved there has to be an acknowledgement of who Christ is; however, there's more to it than that. To validate their point's, people often use a scripture in Romans 10:9, as a supporting verse for this incomplete idea. You see, what they failed to understand was, the Apostle Paul was writing to the saints in Rome; that meant, these were people who'd already gone through the salvation process; which I will lay out for you in just a moment..."

Angelica was a combination of intrigued and appalled with what the pastor was saying. Her interest stemmed from the questions she'd had regarding the subject matter, yet she was appalled because this new idea was dispelling everything she'd learned from a child. She despised the notion of being wrong all of those years.

"...Let's read what Jesus had to say about it in John 3:3-5...Christ Himself advised Nicodemus that in order to see and enter the Kingdom of God, which is heaven, one had to be born again of the water and of the spirit." He further explained to the congregation that being born of the water was baptism; that required full immersion in water. It was the washing away or the removal of one's sins. Then being born of the spirit meant, receiving the Holy Ghost, which according to him was a gift from God. The pastor went through various scriptures, explaining the importance of receiving the Holy Ghost, as it was the Spirit of Christ Himself, residing in the individual.

Angelica found it quite odd to believe that the evidence of someone receiving the Holy Ghost was when they spontaneously spoke in another language. *That's ridiculous*, she thought to herself. *How can I speak a language I didn't grow up hearing or one I never learned? He had me until he said that nonsense.*

She was quite disappointed, as she'd believed that she found a church that would possibly bring her closer to God. But that would be impossible if the pastor spoke nothing but nonsense. *What a shame; and this church was beginning to feel like home.* Out of respect, she intended on remaining to the end of the service, knowing that it would be her last service at New Birth Apostolic Church.

"Now, I'm sure that many of you may be thinking that I'm crazy..." *That's an understatement*, Angelica chuckled. "...but keeping in mind what Jesus said in John 3:3-5, let's now read a scripture in Acts 2:38 – "Peter replied, "Each of you must repent of your sins and turn to God, and be baptized in the name of Jesus Christ for the forgiveness of your sins. Then you will receive the gift of the Holy Spirit." Here we find the fulfillment of what Jesus said in the book of John. When we read the book of Acts, it provides the historical account of the birth of the church. Here we'll find that in every account throughout this book whenever someone received the gift of the Holy Ghost, it was evident by them speaking in other tongues." The pastor then went on to provide a great deal of examples to prove his point. As he provided the scriptural examples, Angelica followed along, taking notes. There was no denying that what he was saying was true. There it was, in black and white, one had to turn away from their sins, be baptized in the name of Jesus Christ and received the gift of the Holy Ghost with the evidence of speaking in other tongues. The revelation hit Angelica like a ton of bricks, and she was beyond grateful for the illumination of her mind to see the truth.

The pastor wrapped up his sermon encouraging the congregation to be saved as outlined in the Bible – "I am not saying that you've never had an experience with God; however, it does mean that you have not completely gone through the process as outlined in the Bible to guarantee your saved. You *must* repent of your sins. You *must* be baptized in the name of Jesus Christ. Mark 16:16 informs us that "anyone who believes and is baptized will be saved. But those who do not believe will be condemned." Christ instructs us to be filled with His Spirit. So don't let this opportunity pass you by. If you are ready to take this step with God, I invite you to come down to the altar, and we will pray with you. If you'd like to be baptized, we'll make the provisions as well."

Several people were heading towards the altar area as the worship singers began to sing *I Need More*. Angelica felt a sense of discomfort about going to the altar, as there were several questions swarming around in her head about the message she'd just heard. There seemed to be an internal battle as to what was true – was it what she was taught as a child or what she'd just read with her own eyes. Angelica thought that the best solution would be to pray, so she lifted her hands and basked in the ambiance of the atmosphere. She began praying out loud that God would lead her into all truth. As she prayed, the sudden urge to go down the altar came over her. She resisted the urge until she heard as it were an internal voice saying, "You need more, Angelica; it's time to make a change."

At the altar, a minister and two other women prayed with her. During prayer, Angelica began to feel a tingling sensation that started brewing on the inside of her. She didn't know what it was, but whatever it was, made her feel like she was losing control. "Don't resist the move of God," one of the women said. "God wants to give you His precious gift, but you've got to let go to receive it. You have got to allow Him in, Angelica. God is a gentleman; He will not force Himself on you. Trust in Him and He'll do the rest." Uncertain as to what part of the woman's monologue was reassuring, but at some point, Angelica decided to take heed to her advice and trust in God. It was at that moment, Angelica heard herself as she spoke in other tongues.

A great wave of joy and peace coursed through her. After the experience at the altar, she was baptized. One of the greeters provided her with a gown, which afforded her to get baptized without ruining the clothes she'd worn to church. Once the baptism was over, she and several others were directed to a room where a young preacher spoke on their experience and provided them with pearls of wisdom that would benefit them through their new journey in Christ. Then the pastor entered the room and greeted each of the new converts.

"Hello. I'm Pastor Charles. And you are?" Angelica gladly shook the pastor's hand. With a smile she replied, "Hello Pastor Charles. My name is Angelica Hunter. It's a pleasure to meet you." Angelica and the pastor continued their conversation. She informed him that it was her second visit to the church. She also told him she believed that God wanted her there since she'd mistaken the name of the church for another church her friend had invited her to. She noticed a frown formulating on his face and asked, "Is there something wrong pastor?"

He deepened his frown and replied, "I don't know why, but I feel led to tell you that you will be facing some serious challenges very soon. But in the process, be sure to guard your heart. And just when you think that the Lord has forgotten about you, He'll show up. So just remain encouraged." He shook her hand again and bid her farewell as he went on to introduce himself to the other converts. *What was that all about?* Angelica thought before grabbing her things and heading out the door.

Bitterness, like cancer affects everything and everyone involved. Cut it out, burn it up, or expire.

CHAPTER

SIXTEEN

A week had passed, and emotionally Angelica was in a complex position. Part of her felt refreshed and revived due to the new found revelation of the prior week. But another part of her couldn't shake the yet to be seen manifestation of the warning Pastor Charles had told her *...you will be facing some challenges...And just when you think that the Lord has forgotten about you, He'll show up*. It was nerve wrecking. It bothered Angelica so much that she called the pastor during office hours, as she wanted him to expound more on his warning. "God is always on your side, Angelica. He won't leave you nor forsake you; however, at times, life's journey would have you to think the opposite. Just be encouraged and don't quit. That is what the enemy wants. So hang tough, and watch God take absolute control of everything. Always remember, this too shall pass."

What was supposedly in store for her was nerve wrecking. *Oh Angie, let it go. It's not that serious. Maybe God wants you to prove* yourself since you denied him so many times in the past. Perhaps that was it; she needed to prove herself and she was determined to do just that. This was feasible. Angelica laughed because her mother often said "Baby, some things cannot be rationalized, but it doesn't make it any less true."

Angelica headed for work. The team believed that they were ready to submit their findings on the top secret project, but first, they wanted to meet and review the information before the submission. When she arrived, she was bombarded by a slew of reporters... "Any news on Londyn O'Conner since she's been found?" "How is Mr. O'Conner taking the news?" "Will he address the media?" She, along with her peers pressed their way through the hostile crowd and flashing lights. Once she got into the building, she was pleased to see that their security team had refused to allow non-employees to enter into the building. Angelica was headed towards the elevators when she grasped what the reporters' questions really meant. *She'd been found! And she was alive! Thank you, Jesus for answering our prayers!* She began to jump and squealed like a little girl who'd just received the gift she asked for. The others in the elevator looked at her oddly, but she didn't care – she could not contain her excitement.

As she headed towards the laboratory, she decided that once the meeting was over, she would visit the O'Conner's and offer them her support. That was the least she could do. Perhaps she would feel less guilty for the damages she could have caused had fate not intervened.

Londyn was unconscious. She felt pain all through her body, primarily on her right side. Her head felt as if it was burning. *Where am I?* She wondered. She attempted to open her eyes, but failed. She heard several voices. None of which sounded like the two men who captured her. *Am I dead? Who's here?* As the questions began to come, she heard a voice. *DJ? He's here?*

"The doctor said that she has a hairline fracture to her skull, and she's been raped several times...she has Chlamydia, and the pregnancy test came back positive." *Who was he referring to? Me? Am I pregnant? No! Not by that...* Londyn attempted to turn her head in the direction of her brother's voice, but that proved to be in vain as the darkness claimed her.

"Officer, as you can see, my sister has not awaken. She's in no condition to answer any questions you may have...how were you able to trace the fingerprints on the envelope to the warehouse where my she was held captive? *DJ? Where's mom and dad?* Londyn wondered before drifting off again.

"What are *you* doing here?" *Why is DJ yelling?* "How dare you show your face here after what you've done to my sister? You're to blame for this nightmare, you insolent dog! Get out of here!" Who is he talking to? "I'm sorry DJ", the person's response was a tremulous whisper. "You've got it all wrong," the woman said. "Get out!" "But…" "I said get out!" *Who was that? And why would she do this to me?* Londyn tried moving, but the state of unconsciousness claimed her yet again.

Londyn didn't know how long she'd been unconscious, but she was becoming frustrated with the way the conversations between the doctor and her family were being conducted. She had questions and since she couldn't wake up, she didn't know if she'd have the opportunity to ask. Then there were the snippets of conversations that elicited a myriad of questions. For instance, why did DJ say their father had a daughter? And who was Cynthia? Was she the one responsible for her abduction? Who was the man that referred to her mother as the love of his life? It most certainly did not sound like her father. *Wake up Londyn!* She commanded, but her body would not adhere to her demands.

A beacon of hope…

SEVENTEEN

Two weeks later...

Angelica paced as she recalled the day she was asked to leave the hospital. DJ was beyond upset...

When *she arrived at the hospital, she wondered whether or not she would be permitted to see Londyn. Surely, only family members were allowed in her room; however, she wanted to show her support. She was reassured that the nurse on duty would relay the message. To her surprise, the family had not placed any restriction on visitors. Angelica concluded that they were probably so focused on Londyn's physical well-being that they overlooked her privacy.*

She cautiously knocked on the door prior to entering. "Hello Mr. and Mrs..." *Angelica halted mid-sentence when she realized that DJ and Aleena were the only individuals in the room with Londyn.*

"What are you doing here?"DJ yelled. He was angry. His eyes exhibited a level of rage that Angelica was familiar with. Not long before, she'd experienced that same level of rage towards her own father. "How dare you show your face here after what you've done to my sister? You're to blame for this entirely, you insolent dog! Get out of here!" DJ charged at her.

"DJ, stop!" Aleena finally intervened. Angelica was glad that her best friend still had her interest at heart. DJ stopped and with a tone laced with venom said, "Get out."

Angelica couldn't leave. DJ was accusing her for what had happened to Londyn. She couldn't leave until she understood why. "DJ, I had nothing to do with this. Why would you accuse me of this?"

He laughed in a menacing tone before he answered, "Oh please. I know all about you, Angelica Devina Hunter. I knew there was something about you that did not sit well with me. I just couldn't put my finger on it, so I had you investigated."

Angelica felt as if the wind had been knocked out of her. What exactly did he find out? "Investigated?" She had to get a grip of herself. She spoke calmly, "DJ, I don't know what you've been told, but I had nothing to do with what happened to Londyn."

"Really? Well we have phone records proving that you contacted one Andrew Donaldson, better known as Patrick. He rented an abandoned warehouse. And it looks like there's no honor among thieves because his business partner shot and killed him, probably wanting whatever money you were offering all to himself."

"The men who captured your sister had nothing to do with me. I had no clue who they were. According to the investigation, the men were mobsters that used your sister as ransom," Angelica attempted to explain.

"Shut up! Don't you dare say another word! I may not be able to connect you to all of this yet, but I know that you played a role in this. I wouldn't be surprised if you were hired by the mob to get close to my family in order to kidnap my sister," DJ accused.

Angelica sighed. She wondered how she could help him understand that she had nothing to do with this. "DJ yes, I did inquire about your sister being kidnapped," she confessed.

"So you admit it!" DJ screamed.

"No, but you don't understand...I was bitter with your father for abandoning my mother while she was pregnant with me. He thought that she'd been unfaithful to him and kicked her out. When I was born, he refused to accept me as his daughter. I was angry when my mother passed away; in fact, I blamed him for her death because she had hoped that he would one day realize that she did not deceive him and that he would return to us. But he never did and I wanted him to pay for what I felt he'd done to her. Londyn was just a pawn, to the man that was my father, but the plan did not go through. You have to believe me; I did not want any harm to come to Londyn. I..."

With gritted teeth, DJ interrupted. "Don't you dare claim to be

a seed of my father!" He placed much emphasis on the word "my."
My father would have never denied his child. It's obvious that your
mother Cynthia, was a whore!"

Angelica gasped. Looking upon his face, his eyes told a different
story, he believed her, but refused to admit it. But how did he know?
"You know, don't you? You had my mother investigated as well. You
know that we share the same father, don't you?"

His hands formed into a fist, as if to control his temper. "I don't
care who you believe you think you are. Whatever issues you had with
my father had nothing to do with my sister! Look at her! She's been
raped, beaten to a pulp, and will be physically, emotionally, and psy-
chologically damaged for the rest of her life. YOU DID THIS TO HER!"

Angelica could not deny that her intent to seek revenge on her
father through an innocent person was wrong. In fact, she could see
clearly now that there was no merit to her intended revenge. Her
mother had provided her with an excellent life, filled with lots of love.
She understood the rage within her half-brother. But she refused to
take the blame for what had happened. Especially since her plan had
not come to fruition.

Angelica sighed, and with a tremulous whisper she said, "I'm
sorry, DJ. But you've got it all wrong."

"Get out!" He barked, refusing to listen.

"But," Angelica attempted once more...

"I said get out!"

Angelica wanted to say something, but knew there was nothing
she could say to reason with him. It was then that Aleena stood and
walked next to DJ. She didn't say a word; she didn't have to. She was
making it clear that she was choosing to support the love of her life.
She'd chosen DJ.

Since that dreadful and awful day, Angelica had not returned
to work. She assumed that she was no longer welcomed at O'Conner
Biomedical Research and Design. She was also heartbroken by the
call she received from Nate. She had called him, hoping that he would
give her the opportunity to tell him her side of the story. She was
certain that DJ had provided his version of the story, which explained
why Nate had not called her yet. She hoped that his feelings for her
would be enough reason for him to want to at least hear her out.
When he finally returned her call, he asked her to never contact him
again before abruptly ending the call. Angelica noted that his tone

was gentle, as if he was ending his relationship with her out of obliga-tion. She was hopeful that God would create an opportunity to mend their relationship. She was in love with Nate and was confident that he loved her too. She wouldn't give up on him.

Although she was distraught from what had transpired, she found solace in the house of God. Church was the only place Angelica felt at ease. It was rather challenging to feel peace outside of the church, as there were constant reminders of what had taken place. In moments like these, she really needed some peace. Angelica de-cided to go to her church. She knew that only the office staff would be there; however, her pastor had always said, "the church doors are always open." Angelica grabbed her purse from the table and headed towards the door. When she opened the door she was surprised to see... her father!

For the record... Life is unpredictable.

EIGHTEEN

"Mr. O'Conner! What on earth are you doing here?" He stood before her in silence. He appeared to be analyzing her. *Why was he here? What do I say to him?* Angelica wondered. She stood there facing her father. Then suddenly fear struck her. *Is he here to hurt me?* Even worst...*is he here to kill me?* She stepped back and was going to close the door when he softly asked "Is it true? Are you my daughter?"

Angelica nervously invited her father in. The conversation was long overdue, but the timing was horrible. She was not mentally prepared for the aftermath she knew would come from their discussion. She was certain that his son had filled his mind with half-truths. But there was no escaping the confrontation now. This was what she wanted, to tell him of the hurt he'd caused her mother, which ultimately hurt her.

"Yes, I am your daughter. Cynthia Hunter was my mother." There, she said it.

"Why did you go after my daughter?" He asked.

Angelica wondered why he had not continued the interrogation regarding her mother. *Did he already know?* She thought it best to answer his question before addressing her concerns.

"I plotted against Londyn in order to get to you. I even sought employment within your company for the same reason. I made you the driving force of my rage because I blamed you for my mother's death. She loved you up until her death." His eyes soften a bit for a few seconds and then returned to their original unreadable state. Angelica continued. "She thought that you'd come back to her once you realized that she never had an affair. She always said that you had and would always have her heart. She never married, thinking that you'd come back. I was so angry, witnessing her disappointment year after year. I then began following your work and found out that you were married with children. Several years ago, I saw a photograph of you and your family in the newspaper and was livid. The headline of the article read *Devin O'Conner: Businessman and Father of the Year*. It struck a nerve in me. I wanted to hurt you then, but my mother wouldn't allow me to even speak negatively against you. She defended you until the end. She wanted me to let it go, but I just couldn't. I now realize that my rage wasn't because of the heartbreak that my mother endured, but it was the hole in my heart due to the father that I wanted in my life, but didn't have. I know this may seem silly; but, all I've ever wanted was a father."

Devin stood, looking at the woman who was the splitting image of him, yet held almond shaped eyes like Cynthia. How could he have not noticed that before? He knew that everything she was saying was true; the investigation he'd conducted, as well as the findings from DJ's investigation had proved as such. He'd even noticed Angelica's middle name – Devina. This was most likely Cynthia's way of giving Angelica a part of him that was unavailable to her.

The past couple weeks for Devin had been horrific. Lillian refused to speak to him and limited his visitation with Londyn. Upon his daughter's release, Lillian took Londyn to her parents' home where she was under constant supervision. He had come clean to Lillian with regards to his involvement with the mob and was grateful that she had not fully divulged all the information to their children, especially Londyn. Devin Junior was obsessed in knowing who Angelica was and trying to connect her to what had happened to Londyn. But Devin knew that ultimately, he was to blame for what had happened to his daughter. Both of his daughters. He was enraged by Angelica's ploy; but knew that her plan had not worked. She seemed to be remorseful and he knew that he was in no position to be judgmental. Had he simply paid off his debt, the mob would have not come after Londyn. Even after her kidnapping, he didn't give in to their threats. He should have just given them the money! It wasn't as if he didn't have it. But not only did feel guilty for what happened to Londyn, Devin now felt guilty for his part in the pain Angelica felt. To know that he had a daughter by Cynthia, the woman he loved, was truly a gift. A gift he'd let slip away from him. It was his own fault his daughters were damaged, and he promised to spend the rest of his life trying to make things right with them. So he planned on starting now.

"Angelica, please forgive me for the hurt that I caused you and your mother. I didn't know that your mother was pregnant and I was never informed of your birth."

"How is that so? When I was born, my mother sent you a letter with the news. You replied demanding that she never contact you again."

Devin appeared confused. "Angelica, I never received a letter from your mother. Shortly after the relationship was over, I moved in with my parents. Your mother knew this..." As if he had an epiphany, Devin sighed and shook his head. "My father..."

"What about your father," Angelica inquired.

"He probably received the letter and sent the response to Cynthia." He continued with desperation in his voice. "Angelica, you have to believe me, I loved your mother. After I told her to leave, I was too ashamed to ask for her forgiveness. I always knew in my heart that she was faithful and often times wondered if my father had anything to do with those photographs of Cynthia with another man. Angelica, had I known of you, I would have come for you and Cynthia. Your mother had and will always have my heart. Please forgive me..."

"What!" Angelica and Devin turned to find Londyn and a bodyguard standing at the door. "You are asking her to forgive you, after what she's done to me?" Londyn was furious. "How could you daddy?" She asked as she came to stand in front of her father.

Before Devin could respond, Angelica spoke. "Londyn, it's not..." Angelica stopped the moment she saw Londyn charge towards her. Londyn punched her, and it sent her tumbling backwards. It was obvious that Londyn wasn't satisfied when she took off a shoe and began hitting Angelica with it. Straddling her, she aimed for her head; but, Angelica blocked every blow with her arms, causing much bruising there.

"Londyn, that's enough!" Devin yelled.

Londyn stopped her assault and looked at the man who was defending the person she believed had caused her so much pain.

She stood. "Daddy, how could you defend this worthless piece of trash after what she's done to me?" Tears began streaming down her face.

Devin came closer to Londyn and wiped the tears that endlessly flowed and said "Baby, she's not to blame for what happened to you."

"But DJ said..."

Devin placed a finger over her lips to silence her. He couldn't tell her the entire truth; not now. "Baby, Junior doesn't know the entire story. Yes, Angelica did plot a kidnapping, but..."

That was all Londyn needed to hear; as far as she was concerned, Angelica plotted to kidnap her and as a result she became a human toilet. And now, her father was actually defending her. Londyn leaped up and slapped her father right before she spat in his face. "You traitor!" She then instructed the guard to hold him. She would deal with him later; for now, she had another matter to tend to.

Angelica's guilt hadn't permitted her to do anything other than block Londyn's previous strikes. She understood her sister's anger and hoped that she would have found some level of solace; however, the new look in her eyes made it clear that she wasn't satisfied. It was then that Angelica recalled her Aunt Tutu's dream...

Angel, I dreamt that a woman wearing a red suit, with black leather gloves, adorned with layers of pearls and heavy makeup had you on your knees. It was as if she was trying to cover up some bruises of her own. You were badly beaten. Your face was bloody and swollen, as if you had been repeatedly hit with the pistol. It was a terrible sight, you were barely recognizable. With tears streaming from your blackened eyes, you begged her to forgive you. She laughed and began to cry. Just when you thought she was going to forgive you, she suddenly stopped crying. Her eyes were as stone; she barely looked human Angel. She suddenly unloaded her gun on you but she didn't want to finish you off quickly. She wanted you to suffer, so she shot you in your left arm, then your right, then your left leg, then your right...

It was as if Angelica's eyes had been opened. Londyn was wearing a loosely fitted red suit with black leather gloves. The gloves did not appear to be one for fashion, but rather used when avoiding leaving any fingerprints. Angelica was in fear for her life and determined that she needed to do something quick! Because her arms had been bruised by the blows she'd received from Londyn, she thought it wise to use her legs. She tripped her sister, causing her to fall to the ground. Before Londyn could react to the surprised attack, Angelica stood to her feet, took off her shoes and was about to reciprocate the attack when Devin shouted, "Angelica, don't!"

The sting of her father's command pained Angelica, causing her to stop. Like a little girl she turned towards him, only to discover that he'd mustered up enough strength to fight off the guard. Devin snapped his head back and instantly the guard released him as he tended to his nose which spewed blood. He then kicked the guard in the groin causing him to stumble to the ground. Turning, he stared at Angelica with extended arms... "Come here."

Overcome with emotions, Angelica ran into her father's arms. This was what she'd longed for; the love and acceptance of her father. "I love you, dad," she sobbed through tears.

Devin was speechless. Although he'd accepted the fact that he had a daughter with Cynthia, he wasn't accustomed to anyone else other than DJ and... "Londyn!"

Angelica released her dad and turned to find Londyn pointing a gun at her.

"Londyn. Baby, don't..." Devin begged.

"Shut up!" Londyn yelled at her father as she pointed the gun at him. "Don't say another word you backstabbing..."

Angelica moved in an attempt to distract Londyn as she feared she would shoot their father. "Londyn! Stop! Put the gun down!"

Successfully gaining her attention, she now aimed the gun at Angelica, who was certain that she would in fact kill her. But she was content with that fact, as she did not want any harm to come to her father – the man whom she'd made the container of her rage. He had turned out to be the missing piece of her once incomplete life. She was at peace with her decision to take his place.

Angelica watched as Londyn slowly pulled the trigger...
Bang!

Epilogue

Four days later...

The tears would not stop. She couldn't believe that her father, the one whom she hated for years, yet became the one she'd yearned for all of her life, was now gone; Angelica was now without a mother or a father. She was all alone in the world. Even her best friend, Aleena, had cut off all communication with her.

Angelica was not permitted to attend her father's funeral. She knew the risk she was taking before arriving at the site, but she'd hoped that she would have been able to pay her respects and remain unseen. She wore dark shades and a headscarf to disguise herself; however, she was stopped at the main entrance by the security. "Ma'am, the family has restricted you from attending this service. Please return to your vehicle."

Angelica remained in her vehicle for the duration of the service, which lasted well over an hour. She imagined that it was filled with tributes, words of encouragement, and music sung by a large choir. She was confident that the family had provided her father with a wonderful home-going in spite of their grief.

She noticed the doors of the church as they opened and turned on the ignition as she intended on paying her respects to her father one way or the other. Once at the burial site, she would remain in the vehicle, respecting the family's wishes; however, when they were gone, she would say her farewell. The pallbearers were the first to exit the church as they carried the coffin containing her father's body. The family followed. Angelica noticed Nate holding Lillian. They were too close for her comfort; however, she knew that Nate was a kind-hearted person and would want to support his friend. DJ and Aleena followed. They looked beautiful together. And in spite of their sorrow, they genuinely seemed to be in love. Londyn was nowhere to be found. This did not surprise Angelica, as she understood the torture her sister was suffering. She had not intended on shooting her father, but she accidently did when he pushed Angelica out of the line of fire.

As the hearse drove off, Angelica waited for the remaining vehicles to follow before tagging along. The burial site was only a few minutes away from the church. Angelica waited in her vehicle until she believed that the coast was clear. She found a tree, which was a great distance away, ensuring that no one would see her. Thirty minutes later, the crowd departed and Angelica seized this opportunity to say her farewell. Angelica stood at the gravesite, staring at the inscription on the tombstone:

R.I.P.
Devin L. O'Conner
(1968 – 2014)
Who knew that angels lived amongst us?

I'm so sorry that we never had the opportunity to establish the relationship that I longed for and what I believed you also desired. I'm sorry for the damage I caused and will continue to pray that God makes your family whole... She continued to pay her respects in silence before vocalizing her last thoughts through tears... "I love you, Dad...Please say hi to mom."

www.ingramcontent.com/pod-product-compliance
Lightning Source LLC
Chambersburg PA
CBHW071304130626
46556CB00003B/1466